T0146394

THE FOUR GUARDIANS

THE FOUR GUARDIANS

Jessica & Jordan Fisher

THE FOUR GUARDIANS

iUniverse books may be ordered through booksellers or by contacting:

iUniverse
1663 Liberty Drive
Bloomington, IN 47403
www.iuniverse.com
1-800-Authors (1-800-288-4677)

ISBN: 978-1-5320-5061-9 (sc)
ISBN: 978-1-5320-5060-2 (e)

Library of Congress Control Number: 2018906417

Print information available on the last page.

iUniverse rev. date: 05/30/2018

THE FIRE GUARDIAN

Long ago there was an ancient civilization called the Children of Geia. They were proud people and very connected to the earth. The Children of Geia are known as angels or demons to the humans that had also lived among them. They are known by these titles because of their beautiful white wings that can appear and disappear at will; although they're called demons because of their ability to use magic, some humans were fearful of the children of Geia that lived in their community. There was also much tension among the humans and the children of Geia for quite some time. One day there was an explosion of anger and a war broke out between the two races, they feared the Children of Geia so they saw it best to destroy their entire race. The war was lost on both sides; there were only a handful of survivors that escaped the bloodshed and scattered around the world of Minemi.

There was often nothing to do in the small cottage that was nestled in the middle of the woods, far from any signs of civilization. Nothing fun at least, in Natalie's opinion. Father was always busy outside in the forest, her mother constantly puttering around doing boring things like washing clothes or tending to the garden.

She was often asked to help, but she didn't like it. She didn't like being in the suffocating log cabin anymore than she liked taking a bath. Instead she preferred to explore the wild, running and playing under the great open sky, venturing off into the never-ending forest as if going on an adventure.

"Natalie!"

Startled by the sound of her mother's voice in the far distance, Natalie leapt forward without a second thought. She knew what would happen if she got caught wandering far from the clearing again. She remembered last time, as the little girl scrambled from the brushes as fast as her little feet could take her, and she couldn't help but tell the similar stern tone in her mother's voice that she had used now and then.

With the speed that surpassed the ability of a ten-year-old, she bounded down the ever-familiar track, past the cluster of familiar tall trees she loved to climb and across the tiny brook that was tinged with a copper color that always had fascinated her. She did not dare to stop though, and hopped from one stone to the next. Even with the risk of being in trouble, Natalie couldn't help but smile. She loved to run.

"Natalie!"

Her heart sank as she picked up her speed in the direction of her mother's voice.

"Here!" She cried when she got closer, hoping her mother would believe that she had only been a minute away. Several seconds later she emerged from the trees and into the small clearing that sat the small cabin where she and her family lived. She could tell by the look of her mother's face that she was not fooled.

"What have I told you, Natalie!" The small woman sighed. "I have half a mind to tell your father. You know better than to wander." She fussed over Natalie and ushered her inside the small wooden cabin. "That's enough exploring for one day. Go wash up and help me with dinner."

Natalie nodded obediently, relieved that she had gotten off easy. She knew if it had been her father, she would never been able to leave the cabin for what would feel like a long time. It wasn't fair.

Natalie didn't understand why it was so bad to have fun. All they wanted to do all day was hunt and clean the cabin, cook, wash laundry in the river - boring stuff that grown ups always did and expected her to do the same. It never made any sense to her that she could not wander farther into the woods if it made her happy. Mother never looked happy scrubbing the laundry against that metal grate until her hands were red. Natalie avoided that punishment at all costs if she could help it.

They had lived in the clearing for a long time now. Natalie could remember a time when they didn't, but only vaguely. She didn't like thinking of those times but didn't know why. She thought back to when they first stumbled on this place after what felt like a lifetime of walking aimlessly through the never ending trees. Once they had settled, the wide eyed girl never stopped trying to wander, falling in love with all the different adventures a little girl with a big imagination could have in the forest. She didn't understand what the problem was, why they had to ruin her fun. They lived there long enough that she never had to fear getting lost.

Grown ups were such worry warts.

Natalie meant to just walk to the river and wash her hands. She knew by the way the sun was just touching the trees that her father would be home soon. Her mother always had a tasty dinner all ready when he returned, sometimes with a catch of the next day, poor creature she thought. She listened to her mothers instructions and put her hands in the water and began to wash up, the makeshift log cabin in sight just like she was told. Then her hands stumbled on the red ball she had thought she'd lost forever and her mother's stern face and firm instructions flew out the window.

She picked up the ball her father had given to her as a gift after he had returned from a long journey. He would be so happy with her when she showed him. He had been pretty upset with her when she accidentally lost it further up the river. She had wanted to see if it would float. It didn't.

The ball was heavy in her hand and the color was not as bright as she remembered, but she didn't mind, she was happy to play with something else other than rocks or sticks for a change. She squeezed it with her little fingers and giggled when small spurts of cold water ran down her arms. She squeezed it again and more water fell and disappeared into the earth. She threw it on the ground, expecting it to bounce like it once did but instead it thudded and rested uninterestingly on the ground.

Determined to make it bounce she picked it up again and threw it harder, water splashing on her legs as it bounced away. She followed it and picked it up. It didn't bounce all that much, not like it used to, but she figured that if she got rid of all the water, it would bounce all the way to the sky. So that's what she did, time and again she threw it, reveling in how fun it was as she chased the ball wherever it led her, again her parents' warning completely forgotten.

She was especially enjoying herself when she discovered the odd dark spots the ball created when she threw it against a rock on the ground. It entertained her for a time but when the ball hit the jagged edge of the rock the wrong way one too many times she grew tired of it. The rocks were very small, maybe if she threw it against a bigger rock it wouldn't bounce in the wrong direction and she wouldn't have to chase it. She thought of a big rock, the side of a cliff she'd passed during one of her adventures. It wouldn't take long to get there.

She was right, it didn't take long. She had entertained herself the whole way along the narrow path, bouncing it against the packed brown dirt, lost to the world and the time passing. Life could be so boring. Her parents never had time to play. If she found anyway to entertain herself, she took it until her parents ruined the fun.

Bouncing the ball against the rock lost it's allure pretty quick. It bounced well now, the water had long been squeezed out of it, but it was disappointing when the ball didn't leave the dark wet spots on the wall of the cliff face. It wasn't fun to toss it and catch it if there was no one to talk to. She threw the ball as hard as she could one last time. The bouncing ball struck the wall with a dull thud and went flying back into the underbrush. Chasing after it, Natalie came to a dead halt.

Natalie had never seen another girl her age before. The girl seemed taller than her, maybe a little older than her too. She didn't have blonde hair and green eyes like hers either and she dressed different; a white gown with weird ruffles at her shoulders, red thread highlighted at the hem and seams. Her eyes were different too the color of mud, like her hair that was pulled back in a long ponytail. Instinctively Natalie knew this little girl didn't pose any threat. The girl had crouched back in alarm like her, her pale hand clutched hard at a branch, those mud like eyes terrified but also a little curious.

"Hi." Natalie said tentatively, as the girl began to back away. She didn't want her to leave. She suddenly felt a desperate need for her to stay.

The girl kept staring, but she didn't run. Natalie took a few steps forward, the odd eyes following her every move. She bent down and picked up the ball a foot away. "I thought I lost this." Natalie said as casually as she could, hoping that the girl would relax and say something. The girl kept watching her but didn't look as scared now.

Natalie threw it up in the air and caught it, then bounced it on the ground. When it rolled towards the silent stranger, between the tall trunks of the trees, Natalie followed it and picked it back up. "Want to try?"

The girl looked at her and then behind her, like she was looking for something as Natalie held the ball out to her. It was like she wanted to reach out and take the ball, but there was something holding her back. After a few seconds, she seemed to reach a decision and tentatively opened her hands. Natalie tossed the ball, and the girl caught it.

She giggled, passing the ball from hand to hand, her tiny fingers exploring the rough surface of Natalie's ball as if she'd never played with one like it before. Natalie smiled too, enjoying the girl's delight in her toy.

"Have you ever played catch?" The girl asked.

Natalie nodded enthusiastically. "You know catch?"

She shrugged shyly. "We used to play all the time at home."

The girl threw it in Natalie's direction, she caught it. She threw it back to the girl but missed. They both giggled as she ran to fetch it. There was something at the back of her head, a tiny voice that replayed something her parents had said; to run away if she ever caught sight of another being. Even though Natalie had this feeling she couldn't place, she dismissed the thought of telling her parents. They wouldn't understand.

By the way the girl kept looking behind her, the uneasy look on her face told Natalie that the girl felt the same way. Maybe her parents told her the same thing. It wasn't fair that she had never had someone her own age to play with. As they went back and forth with the ball Natalie decided that the girl couldn't be bad. She was excited to have a new friend.

"Nice catch!" Natalie beamed when her new friend had to jump to catch it.

The girl smiled back. "You throw good."

"Thank you. My father taught me." The girl threw the ball back.

"My brother." The girl said as Natalie caught it.

"You have a brother?" Natalie always wanted a brother.

She nodded. "Two. Owen and Neil."

Owen and Neil. It would be so much fun to have a brother like Owen or Neil. Natalie passed the ball back.

"I don't have any brothers. What's it like? Do they play with you all the time?"

The girl thought about it for a minute. "It's okay. We sometimes play, but they are bigger and pick on me. They usually just play with each other."

Natalie thought about it in silence as their game continued. That didn't sound like fun. If *she* had big brothers they wouldn't pick on her. They would be nice all the time and run in the forest with her and play catch whenever she wanted. They would stay out until real late and watch the moon rise real high in the sky as they laid by the river. Her parents would never make her feed the scary chickens again or do any chores for that matter because her big brothers would do everything for her.

"Still, that's pretty cool." She said encouragingly, although certain that her imaginary brothers would be better than hers. The girl didn't respond and instead shrugged her customary shrug.

It was a simple game of catch, but Natalie was having the time of her life. She couldn't tell how long they'd been playing for but she didn't care. She could have stayed there forever if the ball hadn't ended up back in the river. Somehow they had wandered too close to the rushing waters and the girl threw it too far to the right. Natalie tried to catch it but missed. Natalie had a sinking feeling when she watched it disappear into the volatile abyss; she had looked forward to showing her father her find.

"Oh no." The girl gasped.

Natalie sighed. "It's okay."

But it wasn't. The girl kept looking in the same direction, like she should leave but didn't want to. With the ball in the river the girl would go back to where she came from and Natalie would have to go back to boring things. She thought about what she could do to make her stay. After a moment she had an idea.

"Want to see something cool?" She asked.

The girl's eyes looked at the direction they had came from and then back to Natalie. She nodded.

Natalie smiled and took a deep breath, suddenly nervous and a little guilty. She shouldn't be doing this, she knew. If her parents found out they'd be furious. If she didn't, her new friend would leave. She chose the latter. She didn't know what the big deal was anyway.

Closing her eyes, she inhaled, channeling the energy her parents told her never to show others. She wasn't certain it would work, but she wanted to impress her new friend with her secret. The girl watched with curious patience as Natalie stood, eyes closed, hand out in silent concentration. One moment it was dim, the sun beginning its descent behind the trees, and the next there was a bright light illuminating Natalie's face as she held a ball of what looked like fire, in her right hand.

Natalie grinned triumphantly when she opened her eyes to the light. She was so new to her abilities and how to manage them. She looked to the girl, expecting to see her face full of awe and wonder. She was confused when the girl did not in fact smile, but began to scream.

Startled by the adverse reaction, the fire disappeared from her palm.

"It's okay!" Natalie shouted, confused when her friend backed away, more terrified than before. She didn't understand, she wanted her to like it. "Don't go!"

She watched as the girl ran away. Tears formed at the corners of her eyes and she wiped them away with angry fists. It wasn't fair.

"Natalie?"

Her pulse raced when she heard her father below in the far distance. She began to run, faster than the girl had. She was terrified, knowing she was in trouble, but she also wanted to run into his arms. That girl was so mean. What was wrong with her?

Her feet flew against the forest floor. It was hard to see with the tears falling down her face, the sun barely visible anymore, but she knew the way and before long, her father's comforting arms were in plain view. Beside him was her mother.

She didn't care that they weren't pleased with her. She kept running until her arms were wrapped around her father's waist.

After a stunned moment, he pulled her away and bent down until he could see her face. "Where have you been?" He asked. He was angry, but that faded away considerably when he saw the tears and her crestfallen expression.

"What is it? What's wrong?" He looked in the distance, taking a ready stance for anything that might be coming from the direction his daughter had come from; casting his eyes from side to side.

Tears began to fall even harder, but she tried to explain. "There was a girl, and she ran away from me."

"A girl?" Her father jerked upright, looking into the dark woods around them with a cautious expression she'd never seen before. He almost looked scared.

"A human girl?" Her mother asked, her tone mimicking the fear on her father's face.

She nodded. It wasn't the complete truth, but she didn't want to get in trouble. She was forbidden to ever use her very new abilities. Her parents would never forgive her if she confessed. She was just starting to understand why they had cautioned her against it but she still didn't understand why that strange girl had to hurt her feelings like that. She hoped she never came back.

She was wrong.

They had started moving swiftly back towards the clearing when the first bark of a dog could be heard in the distance. It was an odd sound to Natalie, but she felt a rush of fear when her parents picked up their pace, speaking in hushed, panicked tones that scared her more than the dogs did.

"We won't be safe there." She heard her father say to her mother. "We need to head west, across the river to lose the scent of the dogs."

He grabbed Natalie by the hand and started to run.

This kind of running wasn't fun. Her heart beat harder than it ever had before, fear clutching at her chest when the howling and growling became more distinct. When they reached the river, her father let go of her hand, her mother ushering her into the water.

They were in the middle of the shallow water when she noticed that her father was not following them, strange shouts and dogs barking so loud now, she knew they were catching up.

"Father!" She cried, as she watched him stand toward the trees, flames licking at his fingertips.

"Hush." Her mother hissed, pulling her by the hand, away from him.

They had just reached the other side of the river when the first gunshot rang. She tried to look, but her mother had clutched her to her chest, letting out a gut-wrenching cry as she watched her husband fall to the ground. Natalie tried to jerk away, she knew something had happened. Where was father?

"Come!" Her mother cried, gasping with grief as she ran with her daughter. Natalie began to cry too as they ran away. The little girl knew he wasn't coming with them. It was all her fault.

They worked their way through the forest, their lives depending on it. Together they dodged trees and leapt over rocks, but their assailants kept coming, the terrifying sounds of pursuit ringing in her ears as they ran for their lives.

Before long she grew tired, her mother too. She didn't know if she could run anymore.

"Natalie, listen." Mother gasped desperately. "I don't think I can go any further. I need you to fly."

Natalie didn't understand. She wasn't allowed to fly. She didn't even think she could again. She had done it once and her parents had been upset, telling her that it was dangerous.

She shook her head, so frightened. She wasn't about to leave her mother behind.

"Natalie." She didn't like the look on her mother's face. "You are going to die if you don't go now. Fly! Fly now and don't look back."

"Do it!" She yelled out fiercely when Natalie still didn't comply. "Go!"

Natalie sobbed as her mother pushed her away and ran towards the angry mob of humans that were now visible in the distance. With all the concentration she could muster with the ragged gasps of sadness that racked her body, Natalie's wings appeared from in-between her shoulder blades and began to lift herself off the ground and towards the tops of the trees with great effort. Eyes closed, gobs of tears flowing down her face, Natalie flew, just like her mother wanted her to. Away from the wretched humans and the only two people she ever loved. Being unfamiliar with flight Natalie found herself unbalanced and descending rapidly unable to keep control. When Natalie heard the gun shots and dogs barking she realized she didn't have any time to waste, and that there were more than just the two people she saw back at the house. Natalie was racing through the woods trying to escape the mob of humans that threatened to claim her life as they did her parents. As Natalie hit the ground she stood up abruptly and blindly ran in the opposite direction of the mob noticing the voices getting quieter and further away.

"Where am I" Natalie said in a questioning tone.

Natalie was completely lost even with the map that her father told her to keep with her in emergencies, so if she ever got lost she could find her way back, which happened to be all the time whenever she wandered too far.

"Now, if I go this way" as Natalie was lost in thought trying to find her way through the woods, she stumbled on a rock throwing her balance off and started to fall down a steep hill.

When Natalie was rolling down the hill her eyes were closed tight and she was screaming in fear. When she landed she found herself hanging in a tree.

"What luck, that didn't hurt as much as I thought it would" Natalie said happily.

But Natalie was wrong, as she said that she heard branches screaming under the protest of her weight. Then she suddenly crashed to the ground in agonizing pane but surprisingly it was a soft landing.

"Hey! What's your problem landing on me, I'm really not having a good day and I'm in a big hurry" said an unfamiliar voice.

"What, oh I'm so sorry, I'm really lost" Natalie said apologetically.

As they both righted themselves Natalie's forehead began to glow a crimson red and a fire marking appeared looking just as erratic as flame itself.

"Well apparently, it's raining guardians, I guess it is my lucky day. Hi my name is Sasha"

THE WIND GUARDIAN

"Where should I start looking now?" as Isaac searched through every town he came across, he found himself in a fishing town with no other trail in site. "I guess I need to ask for directions to the next town" he said defeated.

The town looked run down sitting on sea level; from years of floods the houses had missing shingles and shutters. The houses seemed to curve and make a "u" shape giving just enough room for an outdoor market; the docks were just two meters away from the little town nestled between the woods and the ocean. There was a tree line encasing the whole village with thick brush everywhere; making it difficult to navigate through. Although Isaac could see a mountain in the distance.

As Isaac walked up to a nearby fisherman on the docks he asked for directions. He realised that the fisherman looked old and scruffy with a long gray beard and an arrogant posture to him.

"Why should I answer your question you're just a kid where are your parents" the fisherman said irritably. "You should just go and play somewhere."

Isaac did look like a child but he was a lot older then some might think. He wore a black head band with dark blue jeans and a black shirt with a white coat. His eyes were light silver and his hair was as white as snow.

"Well appearances are deceiving" Isaac said in a cocky tone.

"What was that, are you trying to pick a fight with me you little brat?"

"No just asking for directions. I wouldn't want you to get hurt if we started fighting."

"What was that!" said the fisherman angrily.

"I hope you're not going deaf because I hate repeating myself" Isaac looked annoyed.

"What!, you little punk, I'll teach you some manners."

As the fisherman struck down with his right arm at the boy with all the force he could muster into his strike; the fisherman stumbled forward as he met no resistance from his strike towards the young man. Isaac had moved to the left with one swift motion dodging the punch, and as he did so struck upwards with his right foot catching the fisherman off guard with a sudden impact to his face. The force of the kick was so powerful it had made the fisherman soar into the air. The fisherman was startled by the sudden impact, by the time he realised what had happened he was on the ground nursing his bleeding nose. People started to shout at Isaac and others didn't even know what was going on. The town was in an uproar and Isaac didn't like what came after. The truth is he has been kicked out of many villages because of his short temper and stubbornness.

"Great all I wanted was directions you didn't need to make it difficult. Perfect, everyone always gets the wrong idea. Why am I always the bad guy?"

As Isaac started to run from the angry mob he saw two figures coming out of the woods. "Oh, that's where the trail to the next village is." Isaac was almost to the trail when a frying pan hit him in the back of the head. "Damn, they're all crazy."

As Isaac reached the trail he heard the angry mob following him. The only thought he had was to keep running in hopes that they would give up with the pursuit.

"Finally, I lost them" he said hiding behind a big balky Oak tree.

As Isaac continued walking he came across a rundown stone cabin that looked like it hasn't been used in a long time. Although the cabin still looked sturdy enough to live in, it was also very filthy. As Isaac moved on he started thinking about all the towns he had been to and where he would be able to find his new master.

"This isn't fair I don't want a new master if I have to go through all this trouble. With my luck, the guardian I find will be annoying and hard to understand" Isaac muttered.

As Isaac was ranting to himself he realized that he was completely lost and had no idea where he was.

"Oh great, now where am I? I have the worst luck ever" he said annoyed.

Suddenly he heard crying and went to investigate. He saw an opening in the trees and in the middle of the opening he saw a woven basket. When he got closer he realized it was a baby boy swaddled in silky white cloth. The basket had a handle and on the handle there was a paper star with a black happy face panted on it hanging from a string.

"What! Where are your parents?"

He didn't expect the baby to answer so he looked around to see if he could find any one. "Tough luck kid, no one is here and I can't take you with me. I'm in a hurry and you'll just slow me down" Isaac said apologetically.

As Isaac said this the baby boy looked at him with little white hopeful eyes.

When Isaac started to walk away he saw a faint blue light coming from behind him. Isaac turned around abruptly, just in time to see a symbol of wind blowing on the baby's forehead symbolizing the wind guardian. The symbol was slowly fading away. Isaac stood there wondering what had just happened.....

"Oh, come on! This isn't fair what am I going to do with a child...... "This is outrageous, out of all my bad luck, a baby, you've got to be kidding me" he said kicking around leaves and fallen branches. Sighing with exasperation Isaac stared at the baby intently. "I'm probably the first one to find my guardian because they should all be the same age and I'm just lucky that I get to raise him." stated sarcastically.

Fine I guess I'm going to have to deal with it. So let us start with a name for you how about Levi or Joel..... No, hmmm I know how about Noah. Does that sound good to you, it better. This isn't going to be easy, I bet the other followers aren't having this many problems"

Isaac turned, and as he turned away he grabbed the handle of the basket and started to walk away from the clearing.

THE WATER GUARDIAN

On a cold rainy night there was a knock at the door, the people that emerged from the big white house with two wooden pillars sporting the front entrance creating a shelter from the elements were an old married couple. The man that had opened the door looked weary and had lots of wrinkles all over his face, and had light gray hair. The man was very skinny and fragile. As he looked around to see if there was any one around, he heard crying at his feet. The woman that was standing behind him suddenly pushed her self-past her husband and found a new born baby at their door step. The woman had gray hair and looked like she was as exhausted as her husband.

"Oh my." The old woman gasped as she bent down to comfort the child. "What kind of person would leave a baby in the pouring rain!?"

As the woman comforted the baby she looked down and saw a ragged piece of paper at the bottom of the basket with only one word written on it. As she peered at the paper she realised that it was a name, it read "Zoey"

Ten years later

"Zoey, can you do the laundry for me? I have lots of cleaning to do in the house today" said the old woman.

"Sure, no problem" Zoey said rushing out the door with a bucket of laundry and a metal wash board.

As Zoey left the big beautiful white house she had lived in for ten years she glanced back at her bedroom window that had a gray frame. She loved to have the second floor all to herself with only a storage room beside her bedroom. With her stepparents so old they stayed in the back bedroom for easier access to their living quarters. Smiling at the fond thought of her home Zoey headed to the river. It was a nice sunny day with a light breeze coming through the valley. Zoey loved sunny days especially when she went down to the river because it always sparkled so beautifully like her blue eyes.

"I can't wait for tomorrow, I hope it's going to be nice for my tenth birthday. I love to come back to the water tomorrow and watch it sparkle." she sounded excited as she talked to herself.

Down by the river Zoey saw a strange cloaked person standing by the edge of the river bed watching it flow. As Zoey got closer, the stranger turned around and in that brief second Zoey saw bright blue eyes and short light blue hair.

"A boy" Zoey said confused.

The boy suddenly took off running with the water sputtering underneath his feet with every stride, towards the forest that dwelled near the Meuse river.

"Hey wait, I didn't mean to scare you. I don't have any friends; I was hoping we can talk."

The boy suddenly stopped and glanced back at Zoey with an interested look on his face; then took off running again. Fascinated by his light blue hair and the expression on his face; Zoey went running after him leaving the bucket and clothes behind on the river bank.

"Hey wait I just want to talk to you" she shouted.

As Zoey ran after him he seemed to disappear into the woods. When she looked around she noticed he was sitting above her head on a tree branch.

"I like your blue tinged hair it makes you stand out. So why are you following me?" the boy asked curiously.

"How did you get up there so fast?" Zoey said startled.

"I climbed, how else do you get up a tree" he said sarcastically.

"Ha ha very funny, I asked how you did it so fast" she said annoyed.

"You know you shouldn't be here"

As the boy said that Zoey heard screaming coming from the direction of the village.

"What's going on?" she turned her head abruptly reacting to the noise but couldn't see a thing through the thick trees. When Zoey turned back towards the boy that was perched on the tree he was gone.

"What now where did he go, it's like he just disappeared into thin air." She didn't get much further with that thought when she heard things being smashed and people screaming in pain. As Zoey went running back to the village she could smell a fire. When she got to the clearing of the village everything was engulfed in flames.

"Oh no, what happened!" she said as she started to sob.

Zoey was starting to make her way to her house that was starting to look like it was about to fall over; till she heard voices coming closer and closer. Then Zoey realized that she was frozen in place till someone grabbed her arm and pulled her back into a thorny bush.

"You shouldn't be here" said a familiar voice. Zoey spun around to find the boy that she was following in the woods. As she did so her forehead started to glow blue and the symbol of shimmering water appeared.

"Yeah, I thought it was you"

"What do you mean?"

"I mean you are my guardian, I will serve and protect you, my name is Eli

"Hi, my name is Zoey" she said a little disoriented. What do you mean I shouldn't be here."

"You ask a lot of questions. I mean that if you go over there they will kill you."

"They?"

"Yes, the bandits that are sitting right over there."

Zoey turned to look and saw that there was a big group of rough looking bandits.

"Ok?, now what do you mean by I'm your guardian?"

"All you need to know is that I'm here to serve and protect you."

"But how did you know that I was the person you were looking for?"

Eli gave her a small smile and said "because you followed me."

THE EARTH GUARDIAN

"Well, it's another beautiful day" Logan said happily.

While he was walking down the narrow street he passed a café and thought that it would be nice to be able to have something to eat. Although, he knew that he had no money for that luxurious café and moved on. He then thought that it might be best to go see old Joel, he was the only person in the entire village that cared enough to give him odd jobs here and there. When Logan was turning the last bend in the long road he noticed a cloaked figure watching him, he thought nothing of it, because he was always being watched by people and constantly getting dirty looks.

"Look, it's that homeless kid" whispered a villager.

"Yeah, he's always around here. I can't believe that old Joel puts up with that dirty kid he only causes trouble" An older woman whispered.

"Yeah, I heard that he took a job to build a barn and the next day it burnt down."

"Look at him, he's always in rags his hair is jet black and his green eyes always frighten me it's not normal."

Logan kept walking away ignoring the two women. He knew that it was pointless to care; even though Logan was only ten years old no one in the village liked him for the misfortune that followed him.

"One day I'll get out of this village" Logan whispered to himself.

As Logan got closer to Joel's farm he felt he was in a welcomed environment. Old Joel never looked down on Logan he always treated him like an equal person.

Even though Joel had room for Logan to stay with him at his farm he was too fond of his house, and superstition won over reason. Everyone in town believed that Logan was cursed by the Devil himself. When Logan was growing up he lived in many different homes and every time he got comfortable, the houses and objects started to fall apart all around him, he never got hurt when the places collapsed in on itself. He was standing right in the middle of the rubble every time, he was always the only survivor. After awhile people started to talk and then no one wanted to take him in.

As Logan past the outskirts of the village the farm house slowly came into view, a log cabin with a long wooden porch and a rocking chair nuzzled in the corner near the window of the bed room. You could also see to the left of the house a big red barn that held old Joel's live stock and to the right a big pasture for the animals to graze.

"Hi old Joel what do you have for me today?" Logan asked cheerfully.

"Hello there Logan" He said in a gruff voice. "I need you to fix that darn gate it keeps falling apart and those wolves are prowling around again."

"Sure, no problem"

As Logan was walking to the barn to get the supplies he would need to fix the gate he saw a suspicious person watching him from a distance as he turned to old Joel to tell him there was a trespasser, he realized that it was the same cloaked figure from the market. As soon as he saw him he was gone just as fast as he appeared.

"Wow creepy" he said with a shudder.

When he got the supplies he headed straight to the fence and got to work. When he was done he checked the gate three times to make sure it was done properly. As he finished the days' work and the regular chores he was tired and ready to head home.

When Logan went to find old Joel he was sitting on his rocking chair out on the front porch.

"Hey, I finished all the chores and fixed the fence so I'm going to head home now."

"Good, I will see you tomorrow then and take this too you deserve it." As old Joel leaned forward and handed Logan a basket of sandwiches.

"Thanks, I'll savour every bite." Smiling gratefully

As Logan took the long road back home while eating the mixed sandwiches he didn't take the time to look around for the fear of other kids finding him. There were many people that hated him and the kids that lived in the town hated him the most. When the kids had a chance, they would always throw stones at him and corner him so he couldn't run away the sheer numbers where always against him. With his surprise, when he was walking down the street no one was looking his way and for some reason that made him even more uncomfortable then if people were whispering about him.

As he reached his home he took in the familiar site of the caved in roof and the lonely support beam that was still holding part of the roof up creating just enough of a shelter to hide from the elements. As tired as Logan felt he crawled into a gap that was just big enough for him to sleep in.

Staring up at the broken ceiling he wished so hard to get out of this village to leave it all behind to finally be happy. Sighing out of frustration Logan rolled over on to his side and drifted off to sleep.

The next morning Logan awoke at the break of dawn to alot of loud angry voices shouting and cursing. Logan hurried out of bed to see what was going on; when he got out he realized that there were people with stones, torches and pitch forks.

"Betrayer, Sabotage" screamed the angry mob.

"Wait! What's going on, what happened?"

"You know exactly what's going on kid!"

Logan looked around the mob of villagers and saw old Joel standing there shaking his head with an angry scowl. Logan looked at him with pleading eyes looking for a way out.

As he stood there in terror a rock flew through the air striking him in the head, blood then came streaming down his face and covered the right side of his head.

"Why, why are you doing this" he screamed in confusion.

After Logan struggled to his feet he felt a sharp pain in his side as he looked down to se why he felt a warm sensation running down his side and his left leg he noticed a gash in his left side. It seemed that one of the villagers had thrown a spear at him while he was struggling to get up. As he looked around he realized old Joel was the one who threw the spear and he had a very satisfied look on his face. Once Logan was able to stand he looked at old Joel with tears in his eyes.

"Why have you done this to me." He sobbed uncontrollably.

With tears streaming down his face he asked "you did this to me, but why, I thought you trusted me?"

"I did until you sabotaged my gate and got all my animals killed now I wont be able to make it through the winter."

As the mob continued to throw stones and sticks he sunk to his knees to protect his head and hoped that they would eventually stop and their anger would subside. Although, as Logan cried out for them to stop the mob did not seem to have the intentions to give up and go home. As the beating got worse suddenly a shadowy figure appeared in front of Logan the mob froze in horror as they witnessed the stones and sticks hovering in midair. As Logan herd the angry mob gasp, he opened his one good eye to see the cloaked figure he saw the other day standing in front of him.

"What's your name kid" the cloaked figure said sternly.

"What?, um my name is Logan."

In that instance a symbol of the earth guardian shown as a bright green leaf on his forehead.

"Hmmm, this is interesting, it seems like my hunch was right. Nice to meet you kid my name is Leila."

With her dark brown hair flowing in the cool wind; she stared at him with her Saphire eyes. Logan was shocked at her beauty.

At that moment she turned back to the towns' people and stared at them threateningly.

"If you know what's good for you you'll leave." Leila said angrily.

"Oh really and what is a little kid like you going to do? "

"Well..... I can count how many of you humans are going to need medical attention or worse body bags."

Uncertain on whether or not she was bluffing a villager moved forward and lunged at her with a spear. Leila moved and in one quick motion raised her hand and a wall of rocks came up and threw him backwards making him fly across the street. Logan stared at her in astonishment as the mob of villagers ran away in fear.

"How did you control those stones?"

She looked back at him with a smile. "All you need to know is that you are the child I was sent to protect; and I am your follower."

INFERNO

"Come on Sasha it's this way."

"Are you sure you know where you're going?"

"Of course, I found you didn't I? Um, where are we going again?"

"Yeah, that's what I'm afraid of."

As Natalie was struggling through the thick brush of the forest she suddenly stumbled over a tree root and fell into a murky swamp.

"Oh perfect, I knew that was going to happen, just let me fly you to Geia where it's safe, and it would also be faster."

"Where and what is Geia?"

"Geia is a place of legend. It is a place where your ancestors originated from." "It is also a place where you can't get lost." She said with a sarcastic grin on her face.

As Sasha pulled Natalie out of the swamp and placed her back on the dry ground she warmed her up with a little heat magic emanating from her hands.

"That's incredible how are you doing that, I can only make my hands burst into flames."

"This is nothing to what you are capable of doing"

"One more thing before we go any further, I want you to have this." said Sasha as she pulled out an ember red cloak.

"Ooh that looks so neat it looks just like yours"

"Yes, well now that this is settled, time to go" as Sasha takes off in the other direction."

"I thought we were heading this way" as she pointed to no particular direction.

"You were, I was following wondering when you were going to realize how lost you were."

As Natalie realized she was lost she turned around and started to pursue her follower. Suddenly Sasha froze in her tracks staring out into the dense bush

"Natalie stay behind me."

"What's wrong why did you stop?"

As they stood there they heard a low growl.

"Oh no what do we do" cried Natalie.

"Calm down and think of your element" Sasha said calmly as she pulled out a knife.

"What element?"

"The fire element, you know the symbol that appeared on your forehead."

"Ok? You know I can't see my forehead right."

"Whatever, just concentrate."

While Natalie was frozen in fear she felt a surge of energy and then her body just started moving on instinct. Flames started to form around her, as the flames got bigger the wolves started to back away in terror.

"Good job Natalie you did that without any of my assistance. Now you just need to learn how to control it better."

Just then she looked up and saw a nearby tree in a blaze

"A lot better." Sasha laughed.

Natalie gave her an angry glare.

"Well sue me for trying"

"Well what are we going to do about the fire?" Natalie asked in a worried tone.

As Sasha sheathed her knife she looked at Natalie with a smirk on her face.

"All right lesson number one."

Natalie looked at her confusion on her face.

"You are going to put out the fire you're the one that started it you're the one that has to put it out."

"I thought you were here to help me?"

"I am I'm teaching you how to use your magic"

"Well ok what do I need to do?"

"Concentrate on the fire and imagine it burning itself out."

As Natalie imagined it she felt the heat of the flames die out. When she looked up all she saw was smoke and the blaze in the tree suddenly vanished but she could still see the scorch marks where the fire had been.

"Well done now let's get going."

Then they continued on their journey as Sasha turned away with a satisfied smile on her face.

As they walked they spotted a town that caught Natalie's attention. It was a trading town with many different items and stalls to sell them. The town had many houses and a big town square right in the middle with a tall clock tower over looking the whole town.

"Hey can we go and check out that town over there."

"Well, since you fought that pack of wolves off all on your own you deserve a treat" she said happily.

"Let's head into Stormbourne and we might even stay in an Inn there if we have enough money since it is getting late." As she looked up at the fading light.

Natalie was very excited as they walked through the busy market place. As they explored the town and all the different food and trinket shops Natalie noticed the tall clock tower. Sasha noticed Natalie's interest so she thought to tell Natalie about the history of the clock tower. Natalie was getting bored of the history lesson and began to slowly wander off.

"Hey where are you going?"

"I want to explore the market."

As they walked further down the streets Natalie got excited to see all the different shops.

"Whoooo this is incredible" staring at the shops in amazement.

"What? Have you never seen a market before?" Sasha asked surprised.

"How would I have seen one I've lived in the woods my whole life."

"Well you don't need to get this excited it's just a market"

Suddenly there was a piercing scream and everyone in the market stopped and looked in the direction where it had come from. Natalie noticed all the scared and worried faces in the crowd no one seemed in a hurry to go see what was going on. It didn't take them long to figure out why the towns people were acting this way.

"What is going on, what happened?" Natalie wondered.

"I don't know, but let's go and check it out."

As they ran toward the sound they pushed their way through the huge crowd that was quickly walking in the other direction. When they emerged from the crowd they saw two men in uniforms with jet black swords in their hands threatening a woman at one of the shops. The older man had a big build and towered over the other man who was considerably shorter; he was standing back a few paces looking like if anything were to go wrong he would be the first to run.

"Hey leave her alone!" Natalie screamed.

As Natalie ran forward Sasha followed with her daggers ready.

"What's this, two little girls, well we will teach you some manners and the rules of this town" The older man sneered.

"There is no reason to go threatening people with a weapon." Sasha said angrily.

"This is our town so what we say goes." The younger man said with an air of authority.

As the taller man lunged at Sasha she saw the movement and pivoted to the right. Natalie was so angry she kicked the man's legs straight out from under him sending him flying face first onto the hard cobblestones. As the man struggled to his feet he felt a strange sensation in his right hand that held his sword, it was melting. When the man wasn't looking; Sasha peered over and realized the fire symbol glowing on Natalie's forehead.

"My sword, what did you do to my sword!" The shorter man demanded angrily.

As Natalie and Sasha's attention was focused on the taller man the shorter man saw his chance to escape and ran as fast as he could in the direction that lead out of town towards the woods.

"Come back you fool they're just two little girls!!" The taller man shouted.

"Ya well two little girls just kicked your butt." Sasha sneered.

"You two little girls will pay for this." The taller man said as he backed away from the mysterious strangers.

Then he turned away and ran in pursuit of his companion.

"Well, now that this is over let's go find an Inn for the night." Suggested Sasha.

RAGING WINDS

"Get moving! You're as slow as a turtle" Isaac screamed.

"This is impossible" Noah cried. "If I fall from this height I'll die."

"Then I will have less of a headache."

"That's so cold I thought you cared about me."

"What made you think that?" Isaac smirked.

With Isaacs strenuous training exercises both Noah and Isaac climbed the nearby mountain with 20 lb of rocks in their bags. As they were climbing up the steep terrain Noah noticed smoke rising near the water; as he climbed higher he could see that it was a fishing village with lots of boats heading out for the day.

"Hey why don't we ever go to that village for food?"

"Because you can hunt, and they don't like me there."

"Why is that?"

"If you keep talking you're going to fall"

"I climbed many other mountains and cliffs this one's no diff.....ERENT." Noah's foot slipped on the rocky terrain and started to plummet towards the ground.

"Famous last words; well I guess I have to go save him now" Isaac said irritably with a frown on his face. As he leapt off the cliff after Noah Isaac's wings appeared and he soared after him. As Isaac grabbed him, the weight of the two bags wade him down immensely. Realizing how much effort it took to keep them both in the air and also the extra weight of the bags he sliced the straps of the bags with wind siècles making them plummet to the ground. "You know, you were almost to the top rite? Looks like you're going to have to start over."

"You're joking right..... Right" as a smile faded from his face.

"You should know by now I don't joke" looking very sternly at Noah. "You should probably learn how to take out your wings soon so we don't have this problem."

"So I'm a late bloomer also it wouldn't be as fun for you and you're actually pretty agile for an old man" Noah said sarcastically.

"I'm not old" he spat back.

"You could have fooled me with that white hair of yours."

As they landed safely on the ground Isaac grabbed one of the bags that he had dropped and handed it to Noah. "Now start climbing"

"You're not coming with me" he said disappointingly.

"No, I already made it to the top" he said triumphantly. "Any way I'll be waiting at the cabin for you, don't be late."

"But you didn't climb down the mountain" trying to find a way for Isaac to go with him. "And whose fault is that."

With Noah's last protest he grumbled and started to climb. As Noah got to the top of the cliff he saw the nearby fishing town that he spotted before. "Man, it would be nice to go there for food instead of me going hunting for my own food. Maybe I can take a break before climbing back down, Isaacs always pushing me so hard." as he found a comfortable place to lie down, he slowly started drifting off to sleep.

As Noah lie there listening to the wind in the trees he heard another noise. It sounded like footsteps? "Who's there, Isaac?" As he slowly moved towards cover having his back resting on a base of a tree. He suddenly heard movement above him, as he looked up a net materialized over top of him catching him off guard long enough for the two men that were hiding in the trees to drag him away.

"Hey, let me go" struggling to stay calm "you'll be sorry."

"Oh, why is that, is your mommy going to come save you."

"No,.... Someone much worse" as Noah, trembled just thinking about the devastation that Isaac could cause.

"With your white eyes and silver hair you'll fetch a good price on the black market, and your close look unique with your dark blue pants and light redshirt."

"While they were handcrafted, Isaac doesn't like towns." Noah said dismissively.

As Isaac finished cooking the afternoon meal he wondered if Noah finally finished climbing the cliff. "It's been an hour he should have been back by now. I hope he didn't fall off the cliff again; I didn't spend 10 years raising him for him to die falling off a cliff. I guess I have no choice but to go look for him" sighing with exasperation.

Just as Isaac reached the cliff that Noah and himself were climbing earlier in the day he realized that Noah was no were to be seen. "Were the hell could he have gone, it's one way up and one way down!" In the proses of pulling out his wings Isaac heard voices that were being cared by the wind. The voices sounded desperate and scared and at that moment Isaac knew what had happened to Noah. With a furious look on his face, you could almost see the dark clouds rolling in. Isaac took off into the sky heading for the sound of the voices and saw a pirate ship off to the far cost hidden in a cove. "It's a good thing I can see above the tree line because I wouldn't be able to see the ship through the trees; at least I know now what I'm dealing with." Touching down on the cliff, Isaac made his way towards the trees on top of the cliff. Walking casually into the bandit camp Isaac gazed around looking for Noah; completely ignoring the group of bandits. Isaac notice about fifteen people chained to trees.

"Hey what are u doing here; going to add to our collection" the bandit sneered.

"No I'm going to take from your collection." With an annoyed expression on his face. "Just one; anyway."

"Still as cold hearted as ever I see" Noah sighed.

"I'm here to take back what you stole from me" Isaac laughed. "This is going to be fun. You think you can take from me and get away with it."

"I'm not your property" Noah said irritated.

The other prisoners around Noah seemed to get hopeful but after they heard that the new comer was only here for one person they became somber and sunk back onto the forest floor.

"Well let's get started then" as the wind picked up.

"So you think you can take all of us pretty boy; we have 35 men against one scrawny little boy."

"Please don't get him any angrier than he already is" Noah said petrified.

"Shut up brat" as the bandit went to kick Noah the bandit felt some pane come from his knee and realized that he had lost his leg. Raving in agony he realized there were sickles of wind dancing around the new comer.

"Like I said I'm here to take back what you took from me so don't touch him."

The bandits became enraged and charged towards Isaac. The first bandit got knocked into the air landing in a tree behind him. Isaac looked cool and collected seaming not to move Isaac was so fast the second bandit didn't even see Isaacs fists go into his stomach. As fast as it happened the bandit was on the ground heaving and trying to breath. Isaac had already taken down half the men in the camp with his wind magic just by standing there.

"YOU'RE NOT A HUMAN YOU'RE A MONSTER!" The bandit screamed, petrified blood draining from his face.

As the bandits ran for their lives Isaac notice one still remaining. It was the one near Noah the same bandit that had his leg sliced off and he had a knife held up to Noah's neck.

"I wouldn't do that if I were you" Isaac said in a calm voice with a small grin.

"Oh yeah, why is that, I have what you want you can't touch me without hearting your friend hear."

"Yeah, but I'm not the one you should be worried about. He's worse than me."

As the bandit looked down shaking he notices Noah's eyes glowing white with the symbol of wind on his forehead. Before the bandit had a chance to react a tornado appeared and ripped the bandit to shreds sending him in every direction.

"Well since that's taken care of let's get going" as he sliced the chains from Noah's wrists.

"So why didn't you get yourself out of this situation" Isaac complained irritable.

"You know I'm a pacifist right."

"And we've been through this, you can't be! So why didn't you kill that bandit earlier?" Pointing to the disfigured body parts around the clearing.

"Because he really smelled."

"And you are pacifists, right."

Isaac started to turn away towards home. "You know dinner was ready an hour ago so if you want something to eat you get to eat it cold or heat it up yourself."

"But you know I burn everything I touch!"

"Yeah I'm the only reason you're still alive. With the meals you cook you would have keeled over long ago." Isaac grind.

"Hey, you were kidding about just freeing me right?"

"I don't have a sense of humor you should know that by now."

"Right but let's free them any ways, ok."

"Fine but I'm not babysitting."

THE WATER RISES

"Let's get going we need to get as far away as possible!" Eli exclaimed.

"But what about my family" Zoey cried.

"I'm sorry but the entire village is up in smoke. If anyone is still alive they won't be fore long."

Looking back at the village through the trees the place she called home, she said her last good byes. With the bandits getting closer to their hiding spot Eli grabbed Zoey by the arm and started for the south bridge.

"So Eli, where are we going exactly?"

"We need to meet up with the other three guardians. Then we are heading to the rouns of Gaia."

"What there are others like me?"

"Well yes and no, they are all different in their own way. You can use water to protect yourself wail the other guardian can use there elements."

"Ok so than what's Gaia."

"It's a place where many people once lived and holds many secrets and also many dangers."

"That's great then why are we going to a place that holds many dangers? Why not stay clear of things like that?"

"I will tell you when we finally meet up with all the others."

"How long is this trail to the next town any ways we've been walking for hours?" Zoey complained.

"It's a two days walk from your village Cloudkeep to Spirithold the village to the south. It's getting late we should set up camp." As the sun was setting on the horizon.

As they got to the tasks of setting up camp Eli set up a single tent and then went to fetch some wood for the fire. Wail Eli was busy with that Zoey had walked to a little river that was near their camp site.

"This is triable what am I going to sleep in. I hope he's not going to make me sleep outside with no blanket, it's bad enough that we just left I couldn't take anything with me and now I'll have to sleep outside. Dose he have any shame." As Zoey rambled on to herself wail fetching the water she heard a low growl from the other side of the river. Zoey slowly looked up and noticed that there was a cougar on the other side staring at her. Realizing were the growl came from she started to slowly back away to the comforts of her camp fearing what might happen if she were to scream for Eli. As the cougar stepped closer and closer towards Zoey, she let out a piercing scream in fear. The water from the river sprang to life in the air and started to dance through the trees tossing leaves and branches everywhere.

Just before Eli got back to the camp with his firewood he heard a loud scream coming from the river near their camp. Eli then realized that it was Zoey screaming, dropping the firewood he started to run towards Zoey as fast as his legs could carry him. He notice as he ran that there was water spiraling through the air, and as he got to the river he saw Zoey sitting there startled and completely dry.

"Well talk about learning under presser, and I didn't have to teach you anything." Eli grind and laughed.

"Not funny I could have died" Zoey cried hysterically.

"Let's get you calmed down and wormed up by the fire, of course I have to start it up first." Eli laughed.

As they made their way back to the camp site they settled down and started their fire. As Zoey sat down Eli handed here a piece of dried jerky.

"Thanks, um Eli."

"Yes?"

"If we both go to sleep then who will stand guard, just in case a wild cougar shows up again, also what about the bandits?"

"Don't worry I will stay up and keep watch."

"For the hole night?!" Zoey said surprised.

"Yes I don't need to sleep"

"Hu really why, won't you get tired?"

"Well it's good to stop and rest and replenish my energy but I don't need to sleep because I can borrow strength from you and that's what keeps me going."

"So the strength that you are able to draw from me is like a high or something."

"Well I guess but without the side effects of a hangover." Eli chuckled.

"Ok so you would be able to go to sleep if you wanted to?"

"Yes I am able to sleep, but since we need a look out I will stay up and be the look out."

"Ok then good night." As she started towards the tent that Eli set up for her Wail Zoey drifted off to sleep she started to dream.

"Where am I?" As darkness surrounded Zoey she felt as if she was getting weighed down.

"Who's there?" As the darkness started to subside Zoey noticed a light. It looked warm and inviting, like the fireplace at her old home the one that she would nod off by wail doing her homework. The light seemed to get bigger and brighter till there was no more darkness only light surrounding her.

"Water is ever flowing" said a person in the distance. Zoey could barely make out the person but she could tell that it was a boy with white hair and his eyes seemed to glow like silver.

"I'm sorry, what do you mean by that?" Suddenly the vision changed and she found herself in a small village with a big lake. The lake seemed to have many fish, and the people in the town were caring on with their day as if she wasn't even there. Zoey then heard screaming towards the middle of town and went to investigate. As she got closer she realized it was that boy that she saw before and he seemed to have someone with him. Zoey felt drawn to them somehow like she knew them.

"Mythdale" she heard a voice whisper to her as if it was right beside her. The vision slowly started to fade and she became surrounded by the darkness once again.

"Wait" Zoey screamed wail rising out of bed.

Eli jumped, not expecting the loud scream from Zoey's tent he moved swiftly to the flap of the tent to pear inside.

"Are you alright?" seaming concerned.

"What?" Zoey finally realized that she was having a dream and now notice that she was back with Eli. "Oh, I'm sorry I was having a dream."

Eli looked confused "Did you have to scream, you scared me." Eli sighed and turned away. "Any ways since your up we can pack up and go, the sun is starting to rise. We need to meet up with the other three guardians and there fallowers."

"Right, um... by any chance douse this person have white hair and silver eyes?"

Eli seamed startled. "What? Yeah, but how did you know that?"

"Well I saw him in my dream; it felt like I knew him somehow. Also I heard a voice say Mythdale?"

"Mythdale? That's the town east of Spiritholed, its one days travel from there. Firstly were going to head to Spiritholed to stock up on supplies than were going to go to Mythdale. And if your dream is correct we might find Isaac."

"Isaac?" Zoey said confused.

"Yeah Isaac is probably the one you saw, he does fit the description."

"So you don't know for sure?" Zoey sounded confused.

"Not really the last letter I got from him was 10 years ago and it said he was east from here and he found his guardian. All I can say is there were a lot of anger words, he was pissed." Eli said with a smirk.

Zoey looked confused wondering what Eli found so funny. As they struck camp they headed towards Spiritholed.

"So um Eli, what does water is ever flowing mean?"

"Well water is the element of change. You can craft it into ice, and if you move it fast enough you can also slice through metal at the same time you can make fog for cover so it's both defensive and offense."

As their conversation dragged on they found themselves at the edge of the village of Spiritholed. Before they went further Eli pulled out a dark blue cloak out of his pack.

"Wow that looks so nice it's like yours."

"Yeah it is, it pretty much means were a pair."

"Hu, a pair when did we start dating" she said with her face flushed.

"Hu, oh no I mean... Since you are my Guardian I'm going to need to stick with you." Eli said flushed.

As they made their way into town there was a black banner hanging from the two Towers that formed the entrance to the town. Eli grimaced at the site of it and moved on.

"We shouldn't stay in this town for too long."

"Oh why?"

"Let's hope you don't find out, not right away at least."

"Hey" an unfamiliar voice called out.

As Zoey and Eli turned around they saw two muscular men closing in on them.

"Don't you know you need to pay for entry." The older of the two men said.

"We are just passing through there shouldn't be a fee" Eli said calmly.

"Well, well where's your parents little kids."

"I don't have any and looks can be quite deceiving" Eli said with a warning tone of voice.

"Oh and what is a little kid like you going to do?"

As the muscular man said that Eli's eyes started to glow a bright blue.

"You're both going to turn around and leave, you will not bother us again."

The two men started to calm down and their eyes went blank and they began to listen to Elis words they slowly nodded their heads, so they turned and walked away.

"Wow how did you do that your eyes change color aren't they usually red?" Zoey said ecstatically.

"They change color when I use hypnosis it really only works on people that aren't that smart." Eli said with a smirk "I guess there as dumb as rocks."

"And what did you mean by looks can be deceiving?"

"You ask a lot of questions."

"Asking questions is the only way to learn."

"Yeah but I never hear how is your day going, or the weather looks nice." Eli said sarcastically.

"Okay, okay I got the point but seriously you don't age?"

"That's right."

"How's that possible?"

"Well you can say my growth was stunted."

"Any ways we should get going before those two men come back." Zoey said worriedly.

"Don't worry they shouldn't bother us again we just need to get supplies and leave okay."

"Okay let's go."

As they walked down the streets they saw many different shops in the market. Most of the shops sold weapons and dealt in the black market. Although the market was out in the open they had little to fear because Spirithold was a town that was in the middle of nowhere. Although, there was only one thing missing, the people.

"Where is everyone, there are merchants but the townspeople are nowhere to be seen?"

"This town is dying" Eli said glumly.

"That's awful, but how?"

"Well my guess is, it's the gang that moved into town."

"Hu, gang what gang?"

"Did you notice the black banner on the towers when we arrived?"

"No"

"Well that banner was there symbol no one wants to come out of their homes or there already gone."

"We have to do something" Zoey said frantically.

"It's too late to start an uprising and you're still new at using your abilities, you don't even know how to use them correctly, let's just get our supplies and go."

"Okay" Zoey said brokenheartedly.

As they kept walking down the market square they reached the area where they sold food and provisions most of the stalls that they notice were empty. There were also other stalls that sold camping supplies. There were many other stalls that weren't being used and looked more useful for firewood than for selling goods.

"Hey that stall still looks like it has enough supplies for us." Said Zoey ecstatically. "So what you like to eat"

"I don't eat."

"What... You don't eat, you don't sleep, is there anything else I should know about?"

"Well... I don't age."

"I already knew that."

"Well you did ask me master." Eli said sarcastically.

As Zoey and Eli packed up their things and got their supplies they headed out towards Mythdale. After an hours journey the sun started to set.

"All right lets set up camp for the night we have a long way to go to get to the next town." Eli Exclaimed.

As Zoey tossed and turned in her sleeping bag she noticed with a surprise that Eli was watching her sleep.

"Have you been watching me sleep this entire time?"

"Well I have nothing else better to do."

"Right, maybe next time I'll give you a very long list of things to do." Zoey said with annoyance.

"Well get some more sleep it's still the middle of the night."

LANDSLIDE

"Now that everything is settled down lets head out of town, pack up your things and let's go." Leila said in a hurry.

"Okay, let's go." Logan said excitedly.

"Aren't you going to grab anything?" Leila said confused.

"No I don't have anything." Logan said looking around at all the rubble that he called home.

"You don't even have a little bit of money, or a change of clothes?" Leila said surprised.

"Nope just me, so let's get this journey on the road." Logan was very excited with his first trip out of town.

Leila noticed that Logan was still bleeding from the wound on his side from the sharp branch that struck him. "Hey wait, we have to dress that wound." Leila seemed concerned.

"What oh right!" Logan seems so excited about the journey ahead that he didn't even notice that he was still bleeding.

"Come here and pull up your shirt." As Leila said that, she grab some mud from the ground and started rubbing it between her hands.

"What's that for?" Logan asked curiously.

"It's for your wound."

"I'm pretty sure mud won't help, it will only infect it more." Logan said confused.

"Well yes anybody but you, you can control the earth so in turn it will heal you. Each Guardian has their own element and there elements heal them. The only element that can heal anyone is water it's a pure element. As Leila was applying the mud to Logan's wound the mud started to absorb into his skin healing it completely. So now that you're patched up let's get going.

I want to get out of Sleekshield and head to Falsebrach, that's just to the east of here. We'll stop there to get some supplies and then were off to the city of Zrin."

As they left Sleekshield they headed east but before they got out of the village there were many people cursing and sneering at the two children. When they were out of site of the village Leila pulled out a cloak that looked identical to her own.

"Here put this on it will be better than just wearing those rags."

"Thanks it looks really worm and comfy." Logan thru the dark green cloak over his shoulders.

As the two of them headed towards Falsebranch they noticed something on the path they were on. It looked like it was a big puddle but it didn't look quite right. As they got closer they realised that the puddle they saw was a puddle of blood, and found that there was a carriage wreckage off to the side of the trail.

"Bandits!" Leila said uneasily

"Bandits? I didn't know there was bandits in this area." Logan said frightened.

"Usually not, they mostly like to stay near their camp."

"Where's there camp?"

"Their camp moves from place to place but the target always satays the same, they like to stay close to Zrin's trade routes but they never come this far south. I'm afraid that these people had something very important that they were carrying." Leila said concerned.

"Were would they be heading on this rout there's only one town they can get to on this road and that's Sleekshield." Logan was confused.

"No, you can get to Blufron from here; but it takes three days to travel it, although it is the safest rout but not too many people know about this path it's very well hidden."

"I wouldn't want to stick around and find out what exactly happened here, let's get going."

"Ok."

"HELP..." A choked whisper came from the carriage wreckage.

"What, I think I heard somebody; maybe someone's still alive over there." As Logan raced off towards the carriage wreckage he saw an old man clinging to life. It seemed that he was pinned between the ground and the carriage. The man's eyes looked hopeful at the site of the young boy.

"Please, take this and keep it safe." As the old man raised his hand he produced a lite blue crystal. As he safely handed it to Logan the old man took his last breath and passed away.

"What is this?"

"Logan are you alright, where are you?" As Leila came up behind Logan she noticed the light blue crystal he held in his hands. "Hey, what do you have their? It looks familiar to me."

"The old man just gave it to me. He said to keep it safe."

"All right we need to get going I think this is the object that the bandits wanted if so we need to get out of here as soon as possible." Leila said distraughtly.

As they continued on their path Leila was even more cautious of their surroundings and was anxious to get to the next town. Leila knew if she had to fight she would not be able to keep Logan from creating an earth quake, and bring down half the forest with him being untrained and unexperienced. As they got to the next town without incident they began to look around for supplies and clothes for Logan. Although something seemed strange in this town, the town looked deserted with doors and windows broken in and signs that once hung from the buildings now lettered the streets.

"Let's grab what we need and go!" Leila said anxiously. As Leila spotted a clothing stall she grabbed a light gray T-shirt and black jeans that looked like it could fit Logan. They ran to all the stalls looking at what was left behind in the bandit raid. Grabbing containers of food and other little ration packs, Leila picked up some camping supplies with a sleeping bag and matches to start their camp fire.

"I hope you're ready because were leaving." Leila said hurriedly. "This place is giving me the creeps and I feel like were being watched."

As they rushed out of town Leila breathed a sigh of relief knowing that there was no immediate danger.

"Finally were out of that ghost town, although we went straight into the hornets' nest." Leila said bitterly to herself. "Okay let's see what you can do and what we need to work on. Since we came across a few places where there seemed to be bandit activity I should probably train you on the basics. Let's start with moving a rock around those trees making sure not to hit them and remember you have to stay as sturdy and hard as a rock."

As Logan slipped on his new outfit pulling on his gray T-shirt and blue jeans; as he started towards a boulder close by Logan bundled up his rags and through them to the ground. "Right, I can do this just need to concentrate right?" Logan seemed excited about the test but also uncertain.

As Logan stood firm he felt a pull deep within his sole, tapping into it he suddenly realized that the rock in front of him started to float into the air. Carefully and slowly he started to maneuver the rock around the trees further from him, and carefully guiding it with his hands. As he got to the end of the tree-line Logan slowly reversed the rock and started pulling it towards him slowly maneuvering it back through the trees. Leila stood there amazed at the control that Logan had over the rock. As Logan finished his test of control over the earth he jumped up in excitement raising his hands in the air. "All right I did it, did you see that it was awesome!" Although as Logan lifted his hands the rock followed the action and went straight through the tree line and into the cliff side.

"Oh shit!" Leila said horrified.

The boulder that hit the mountain caused rocks to bring down a land slide. Leila screamed and held up her hands to stop the rocks from crashing down on them. There were so many boulders falling off the peak of the mountain it was all she could do not to flinch with every rock that came crashing towards them. Slowing the boulders down just enough; making them fall harmlessly to the forest floor. As Leila breathed a sigh of relief she noticed that Logan was gone.

"Logan, where are you? It's okay I stopped the rocks and it was your first time, you don't need to hide, and I'm not mad at you."

Realizing that Logan wasn't anywhere close by Leila decided to look around taking note of where he was standing before the rocks came down. With fear coursing through her body she noticed that his footprints stood firm but then she also noticed that there were scuff marks in the dirt that showed that he was pulled backwards. Looking further into the bushes Leila found several other sets of footprints leading towards Zrin.

"This is so bad, how can I have lost him already. Okay it's not too bad I just need to follow these tracks they will lead me straight to him, yeah right straight into trouble." Leila said irritably "well at least they are bringing him in the direction we need to go."

THE LOST GUARDIAN

As Sasha left the Apex inn she went out in search of Natalie. Natalie had been sent out to go shopping and had been gone for almost 2 hours.

"Where could she have gone, it's taking too long just to do some shopping?" Sasha said annoyed.

Suddenly Sasha hared a faint whistling in the distance and knew it was Natalie. Since Natalie had a habit of getting lost Sasha had the foresight to give Natalie a whistle so even if she did get lost Sasha could find her easily.

"Well I better go get her." As Sasha started to run towards the sound of the whistle.

Weeding her way through the crowd of people she noticed that the sound of the whistle went even further than the border of the town and into the woods. As Sasha got closer to the sound of the piercing screech of the whistle she noticed Natalie standing in a clearing underneath a big oak tree near a small pond.

"All right, all right I'm here you can stop blowing into that damn whistle. I'm wondering if it was good idea to give it to you, although I did find you quite fast which is good."

"Sasha, I'm so glad you're here." Natalie said happily.

"How and why are you way out here? You know the markets in town right." Sasha said frustrated.

"Well yes of course, but I met this nice man and he said he wanted to show me something. Although when we got out here he was being quite pushy. Then he scared me and well um... I kind of set him on fire." Natalie said embarrassed.

"You set him on fire." Sasha said in disbelief. Sasha looked around expecting to find ashes of what once used to be a person but couldn't see anything of the sort.

"Well it was an accident but he jumped into the pond and ran away; I never seen someone run so fast." Natalie said amused.

"Well since your safe let's start heading to Mistkeep village."

As they started to tread through the woods back to the main trail they heard a faint noise in front of them. A man had been standing in the brush just ahead of them and as he stepped out to greet them they notice that he had second degree burns all over his body and his close look like they had seen better days.

"Hey I know you." Natalie said surprised.

"You should, you almost killed me you brat."

"It was an accident." Natalie screamed trying to convince everyone of her innocence.

"You are going to pay for what you did to me."

Suddenly Sasha and Natalie became aware of the other man hidden in the trees. Threateningly holding pitchforks and stakes with hammers and also, wearing garlic around their necks.

"Um, I'm not a vampire you know." Natalie said with a deadpan expression.

Slowly moving to the side Sasha guided Natalie to the path they needed to take inching farther and farther away. As the angry man lunged at the two girls they took off running north to Mistkeep. Although their efforts were in vain; they were surrounded by men all around them.

"Fine, I guess I have no choice; you should have just let us go. This will be your second mistake of the day." Sasha finally had enough of the morning events and wanted nothing more than to be on their way. She started to concentrate on the heat of the morning sun feeling the warmth of it; suddenly the temperature started to rise steadily. The men started to back away and some even fell to the ground trying to crawl away but they could no longer spare the effort to move or breathe. Sasha was burning out the oxygen in the air around them and making the men who threatened them fall to the ground unconscious.

"Well that should hold them for a while, let's get going shall we."

For the sixth time that afternoon Sasha listen to the blaring notes of the whistle. Natalie had been sidetracked by many different animals throughout the day and had followed them off the trail and into the forest losing her way and having to resort to the whistle that Sasha had given her. As Sasha spotted Natalie she noticed that she had a bouquet of flowers in her hand that were many different colors. "What! You went flower picking this time; well at least it wasn't an animal carry you away." Sasha said annoyed. Sasha grabbed Natalie's hand and brought her back onto the main road. "For the last time stay on the path." Sasha said frustrated.

"Okay, I'm sorry it's just so interesting."

"I don't care the next town we come to I'm going to buy you a leash maybe then you will stay with me." Sasha said in a series tone.

"Okay, I'll pick flowers on the side of the path."

"Fine, just keep up with me okay."

As Sasha walked further down the trail she noticed something strange about the ground it looked like it was recently unearthed and covered with different gravel and sand leaving it looking out of place. "I wonder why someone would put a pitfall here and who would be stupid enough to fall for something like this."

"Sasha look at all the pretty flowers I found. There nothing like the ones that grow near my place at all." As Natalie strode up beside Sasha she could see all the pinks, purples, yellows, and blues in her bouquet of flowers.

"Oh look Sasha a stream didn't you say there was a stream near the village." Natalie said as she started to run towards the river.

"Wait Natalie it's a..... Trap." As Natalie fell into the pit her bouquet of flowers streamed everywhere with the pinks, purples, yellows, and blue petals fluttering above the pit. "I rest my case there is someone stupid enough to fall for it. Well at least she stayed on the trail."

"Natalie are you okay? Are you still a live down there?"

"That hurt." She said in a muffled voice.

"How do you fall for something like that?"

"I don't know but can you please help me out of here."

Sasha looked around for something that she could use as a rope to pull Natalie out of the hole. Sasha noticed a coiled rope sitting just in the bush that was beside the hole. "It seems to me someone put this pitfall here just to piss people off." Sasha said in disbelief. Sasha lowered the rope down to Natalie and with hasty hands Natalie tied the rope around her waist and slowly was pulled out of the hole.

"You need to be more careful" Sasha said while pulling Natalie out of the pit.

"I didn't see it there."

"No kidding!" Sasha sighed in exasperation. "You're unbelievable, I can't keep my eyes off you for a second."

Moving slowly around the pit that covered the entire trail making sure Natalie stated above ground and not below. They made their way to the River that was about 20 feet away from the walls of Mistkeep. As Sasha bent down to replenish their supply of water she took her eyes off of Natalie which seemed like to be only seconds and when she went to hand Natalie her canteen of water she was gone.

"Are you kidding me, that's it I'm getting a leash for her!" Sasha said furious.

As Natalie moved away from Sasha she noticed a black cat wearing a red color and a bell. Natalie had always liked animals and this cat looked like it belonged to someone so she decided to chase it and she went further and further into the forest following the mysterious black cat. The cat seemed to have disappeared as she was trying to follow it and realized how lost she was when she looked around.

"Oh no, Sasha's going to be so mad at me now." With a horrified expression on her face.

As Natalie tried to remember which way she had come she noticed the smell of a campfire. Before she could venture any further towards the smell of the campfire she felt something hit her head hard and fell to the ground. Before blacking out she noticed a group of people but all she could see were their feet, and then there was nothing but darkness.

When Natalie woke, she noticed she was lying in an old Rusty Cage. Looking around she noticed many other cages around her looking just as unclean and rusty as her own cage. As she took in the view of her surrounding area she noticed she was in a bandit camp, and at the same time she noticed a boy with black hair and glowing green eyes. He wore a light gray T-shirt and dark blue jeans and looked like he had been in the cage for about a week. Since he had a black eye and blood running down his face and also many bruises all over his body. That is to be expected in a bandit camp since you're the bandit's property once you're in their camp.The boy had noticed her movement and realized that she was staring at him with her green eyes and her blonde hair looked matted with dried blood. "So, what are you in here for?" The boy said sarcastically.

ISAACS' RAMPAGE

"Noah get up I've been trying to get you up for an hour now." Isaac said annoyed.

As Isaac left the bedroom he grabbed a bucket that had been left by the counter in the kitchen, since they had no running water in the cabin Isaac went to the well that was just out in the front of the yard. The well was nuzzled between two shrubs and just a few feet away from the cabin. Heading towards the well Isaac filled the bucket with the icy cold morning water and headed back towards the cabin. As Isaac got to the door of the cabin he passed through the kitchen looking determined to wake up Noah. As he got to Noah's room he realized that he was still sleeping soundly in his dry covers. Isaac had a devilish grin on his face knowing that he wouldn't be dry for long.

"Noah this is your last chance to get up. One... Two... Three." Isaac dumped the entire content of the icy cold water onto Noah.

"Mmm......" Noah groaned and rolled over.

"Get up!" Isaac sounded frustrated now. Isaac brought up his foot and kick Noah so hard he fell out of bed and onto the floor.

Noah seemed dazed and wondering why he was so wet, cold, and on the floor.

"What's wrong Isaac, why do you look so mad, and why am I on the floor?"

"Get up we need to get going now!"

"Why?"

"Because you are old enough now to meet up with the others and on top of that the bandits that were left behind will probably come back for revenge. If they ever get the nerve." Isaac said as he was rummaging through the cabin grabbing anything that they might need.

"All right I'm up I'll get packed and ready to go." Noah said groggily.

"I packed a bag for you just get up and change." Isaac said as he stormed out of the cabin grabbing two water containers and headed back towards the well.

As Noah took to the task of pulling himself out of bed and changing into a dry new outfit he heard Isaac muttering to himself angrily.

"Okay I'm ready where are we going?"

"Finally we need to start walking, let's go."

"Okay but where are we headed?"

"To find the others."

"Thanks, I was asking where's the meeting place?"

"We are headed to Zarin and on the way we will be stopping in Mythdale for more supplies. I hope we have enough supplies till we get there it's just too the West of here."

"Isn't there just a town south of here just out of the woods?"

"Yeah but they don't like me there."

"We've never been out side of the woods?"

"You haven't, but I have. Since you were only an infant I didn't know how to take care of you so I went to go ask for advice and well my temper got the best of me. I'm afraid if we go back there we might be burned at the stake."

"What did you do to make them so mad at you?"

"Well I kind of used my wind magic and lifted this middle aged man into the air. I found it hilarious he was screaming and calling me nasty names. On the other hand the townspeople didn't like it so much." Isaac laughed remembering that moment. "He got all up in my face when I asked his wife how to take care of a child I don't know why he got so angry, it could have been that I was standing too close..." Isaac trailed off.

As they made it through the woods they past Kilmire the town Isaac refused to go to or anywhere near there for that matter. They started on to the road towards Mythdale. Being cautious of their surroundings making sure not to get ambushed by any unsuspected enemies Noah began to move the wind around the trees using it as a second pair of eyes like a bat sonar but with wind.

"Well done you should always take every opportunity to practice and hone your skills."

Realizing that the area was clear Noah took off into the air 4 feet off the ground hovering with the wind underneath his feet. Noah seemed so distracted having fun hovering up and down on the wind that he didn't notice someone coming up the trail. Isaac however did and the action he took sent Noah sprawling on the ground. Isaac had summoned his wind magic and forced Noah to the dirt road.

"What was that for?" Noah groaned in pane.

"It was the only way I could think of getting you back on the ground fast enough without yelling at you and notifying are new arrival." Isaac said cautiously.

"What? Oh my bad, sorry."

As the man came closer they realized he was a traveling merchant with his handcart that he polled behind him. Suddenly the merchant noticed the two travelers staring at him grasping his perfect opportunity that he saw in front of him he jumped into the chance to sell some of his fine goods.

"Well, well, I see you two look like you're in the mood to shop and browse just look at all the wonderful items I have in stock."

Noah was impressed with the merchant he seemed to brighten up so quickly even though he looked tired from his travels. As Noah looked at the merchants' unusual items that seem to be from different parts of the world and from other cultures he noticed a small green crystal that caught his eye. Isaac on the other hand wasn't impressed, he didn't like it when people pushed things on him and merchants were very pushy. "Sorry were not interested." Isaac sneered.

"Wait, Isaac look at this." Noah picked up the glowing green crystal and passed it to Isaac.

"On second thought, how much is this?" Isaac wondered.

"Oh that is very valuable and rare." The merchant seemed to be very knowledgeable. "This item is worth $1000.00."

"You're kidding, for this thing." Isaac seemed dumbfounded. "You don't really know what this thing is do you."

"Well... Of course I do... Why do you think it's so expensive?" The merchant stumbled on his words.

"Of course you do, but did you know that there are only four crystals in the entire world like this."

The merchant saw his chance and pounced. "You see if there are only four in the entire world it must be very valuable..." The merchant trailed off as Isaac started to talk.

"Just because there are only four doesn't mean their valuable. To you it's a piece of worthless rock. So how much is it?" Isaac seemed stern.

The merchant wasn't convinced of what Isaac had told him but he was also aware of Isaac's tone. The merchant didn't want any trouble but he didn't want to be robbed either. "I told you it's $1000.00 for this crystal." He stuttered on his words trying not to show Isaac that his glaring was making him fearful of what he might do. Isaac moved closer to the merchant and whispered into his ear so only he could hear.

"Or we can just do $100.00 and we can call it even." Isaac said in a venomous tone.

"What! How would you call that even?" The merchant was taken back by these words.

"Your still in one piece, are you not." Isaac stared him down as the wind started to pick up at his feet.

"Here, here, just take it." The merchant pushed the green crystal into Isaac's hand and started to pull his handcart away from the unpleasant traveler, but not before Isaac slipped the money into the merchant's pocket.

"Well you can be nice at some points." Noah said happily. Obviously Noah didn't hear the conversation between Isaac and the merchant.

"Well merchants need to make their living somehow."

"So how are we going to get supplies in Mythdale if you spent all our money?"

"Will manage." Isaac said dismissing the matter.

"Maybe you will but I still need to eat." Noah said bitterly. "So what's so important about that crystal you had to give all our money away?"

"I'm not sure, I know it's priceless to us and finding it so easily like this it was an opportunity I couldn't pass up."

"So let me get this straight you bought a crystal and spent all our money on it just because you think it will be useful to us."

"Yeah, pretty much."

"Well I guess I'm starving then." Noah said bitterly.

"Let's get going we still need to get to Mythdale." Isaac dismissed the thought.

As they walked through the woods to the next town they were fortunate enough not to meet up with anyone unpleasant. Although it would also be unfortunate for anybody to stumble into them. Even though Noah said he would become a pacifist he was very upset about Isaac spending all their money on something so worthless. Usually that would mean Noah would have to fend for himself, that didn't really appeal to him in the least. With Noah in such a bad mood, if anybody were to approach them at this moment Noah thought he might snap.

"Finally we made it to Mythdale, now all we need to do is find work so we can get more money. This way we could spend the night in the inn." Isaac said gratefully.

"When you say we go find work you mean me don't you." Noah said with a sickening feeling in his stomach.

As they reached the inside of the town Isaac and Noah split up to look for work. Asking everyone they came across if they had any work available. They soon found themselves at the waterfront, talking with a woodworker that crafted small wooden boats to use for fishing in their small village.

"Yeah I could use some help, I need two more boats made before the end of the day." The woodworker said happily.

"Great, let's get to work than." Noah said happily finally being able to earn some money for their supplies they would be needing.

"Well good luck with that, have fun." Isaac said while turning around and walking away.

"Wait, this will go a lot faster if you help, please Isaac you at least owe me that." Noah said pleadingly.

Isaac looked at Noah with a distasteful attitude "you're really going to make me help you earn your own money."

"You're the one that spent all the money." Noah said annoyed.

"Fine, I'll help but this is the last time." Isaac groaned.

Getting to the task of slowly crafting the wooden boats by hand using chisels and sand paper to smooth out the edges of the boat. It was finally getting close to the end of the day and Isaac and Noah were exhausted with the days' work they were done with painting, carving, and building the boat.

"All right, we're almost done all you need to do is go pick up some supplies for me in town square. That shouldn't take too long then I'll pay you for your work today." The woodworker was happy to be done before the sunset that evening.

"Sounds good." Noah was happy to be finished their work for the day and couldn't wait to sleep in a nice comfy bed.

"All right then let's get this over with." Isaac sounded irritated although it's not much different from how he usually acts Noah thought. As they made their way into town to pick up the supplies for the woodworker they started heading back through town square. As they were passing through a crowded area that was near a clothing stall there was a lot of pushing and shoving going on to get at the good deals that the shop owner was offering. Suddenly Isaac got shoved from behind and dropped the box of supplies all over the ground.

"What the hell's your problem?" Isaac exploded with anger and turned around to punch an unsuspecting man in the face. The man was then on the ground nursing his broken nose. Isaac then had a flashback of a similar incident at another fishing town about 10 years ago. Everybody started to scream and yell at Isaac.

"Well now I know why you don't like to go into towns." Noah said sarcastically.

"Isaac?" A voice came out of the crowd.

Isaac looked over to where he heard his name being called and saw a boy with red eyes and light blue hair and was very easy to be spotted out in the crowd. He had a black shirt and blue jeans and wrapped himself in a blue woolen cloak.

"Eli?" Isaac was surprised.

Amazed to find Eli standing in the middle of town. As Isaac looked over he noticed a young girl standing beside him with blue eyes and brown hair. This girl wore a white T-shirt and a light blue skirt and also wrapped herself in the same blue woolen cloak.

"Getting into trouble as always I see." Eli said with a grin.

THE CROSSING

As the four companions sat together around the table at the Double Lion Inn they became more acquainted with one another.

"So Isaac, are you older than Eli?" Zoey was curious.

"No, why do you ask that?"

"Because your hair color is white. Why is your hair white if you're not old?"

"It's white because its white now shut up and drop the subject." Isaac said irritably.

"You know, you could be a little nicer." Eli chimed in. "So how did you find Noah." Eli looked at the silver haired boy with his bright white eyes.

"I found him in the woods, abandoned so I raised him." Isaac said bitterly.

Eli started laughing hysterically. "I didn't have to do that I was smart about it."

"What do you mean you were smart about it you didn't have to raise the kid." Isaac sneered.

"I was smart because I left her at the doorstep." Eli looked smug.

"You did what, then how is it that you didn't know who I was when we first met." Zoey said furious.

"Calm down, I was sometimes watching and at other times I was out doing work getting money so when it was time for us to travel I could buy you things that you needed. Also you grew up a lot so I wasn't sure if you were the girl I left at that doorstep that night or if you were someone else."

"You didn't want to share your bright idea with me." Isaac interrupted.

Eli looked over and smiled at Isaac. "You would never listen to me anyway."

"You didn't like spending those 10 years with me?" Noah seemed disappointed.

Isaac glared motionless at Noah. "What do you think?"

"You're right, I'm surprised I survived those 10 years." Noah shivered at the thought of the intense training sessions Isaac putt him through.

"Well since that pleasant conversation is over you to should get to bed, we have a long way to travel tomorrow. Eli exclaimed.

"Where are we going?" Zoey wondered.

"Were heading to Cloudpond just to the south of here and then were going to take a ferry from Cloudpond to Shimmer Cliff."

As Eli and Isaac headed downstairs to the tavern leaving Zoey and Noah in the bedroom where they had a sheet draped over a rope that they had put across the room to separate the two beds that were placed there.

"Well I hope the journey will go well." Eli said hopefully.

"Just stay out of my way and it will be."

"Well you're pleasant as always."

"I just want to get going waiting for them to sleep to regain their energy is frustrating." Isaac said bitterly.

"It may be frustrating to wait but without their energy we wouldn't last too long on this trip either." Eli said cautiously.

"Yeah, well nothing we can do but wait now." Isaac said frustrated and grumpy.

Eight hours later Isaac stayed comfortably nuzzled in a corner knowing farewell that it would be sometime before Noah would be up. Sitting in his corner Isaac listened to the sounds of feet going up and down the stairs he noticed the sound of a light pair of footsteps coming down the stairs.

"Must be the water girl." Isaac mumbled to himself.

"Hey Isaac when are we leaving?"

Isaacs' eyes shot open in surprise he wasn't looking at Zoey who he thought he would see it was Noah.

"You're up?"

"Yeah I'm up why wouldn't I be?"

"Because of your heavy sleeping I could never get you up in the morning. Have you forgotten the morning I had to dump water on you?"

Eli sitting not too far away tried to suppress a laugh. "You dumped water on him that's one way to get someone up."

"Yeah it is but it also didn't work."

Eli then chose that moment to laugh out loud. "So it's that bad; you must have had a fun time training him."

A little while later Zoey came down to join the other three for breakfast. "Good morning." Zoey said cheerfully.

"You sound energetic, are you excited for the trip." Eli wondered.

"Yeah, since you told me were going to be headed across the water on a ferry I can't wait."

"Typical, the water girl loves the water. What's so exciting about that?" Isaac said annoyed at how much energy Zoey had overwater. "Here's a glass of water be happy." Isaac shoved a glass of water towards Zoey.

"I'm excited because I have never been out of my hometown. Also I love the water and I haven't been on a boat before." Zoey shot back.

After breakfast they all packed up their belongings and left the double lion Inn. Although before they could get on their way they were stopped by 10 muscular man. They looked ready to smash some poor guy's face in unfortunately for Isaac they were.

"Hey you're the kid that punched my brother out he has a broken nose because of you." The muscular man said angrily.

"Well then maybe he should watch where he's going." Isaac said with a deadpan expression.

"Don't provoke them Isaac we don't need any trouble." Eli scowled.

"Your friends' right but we came looking for trouble so prepare to get put in your place little kid."

"What did you call me?" Isaac said with a deadly look in his eyes.

"I said little....."

Before the muscular man could finish Isaac jumped high enough in the air to reach the man's head in a split-second the man was on the ground trying to catch his breath and wondering what happened; what he didn't notice was that Isaac used his legs to get close enough to send him flying back with a powerful kick below his chin.

"You shouldn't have called him that." Noah said shaking his head.

The other men stunned by what just happened shook themselves out of it and started towards Isaac. Isaac was ready to fight the angry mob but all of a sudden he felt a pull from behind it took him off guard and he found himself being dragged out of town and into the woods.

"Hurry run let's get out of here if they catch us well be here for a wail." Eli exclaimed.

As they safely got out of town and far enough into the woods Eli dropped Isaac and they all stopped to take their breath.

"What was that for I could have taken all of them?" Isaac yelled at Eli.

"You probably could have but then the entire town would have been after you." Explained Eli.

"Why would they even be after me I'm not the one who started it." Isaac shot back.

"It's because they're all from the same community they don't like outsiders beating up on the townspeople." Eli said exasperated.

"Any ways that aside let's get on the road to Cloudpond the boat will be leaving in two hours' time." Eli said looking at the two guardians. "Maybe while were heading to Cloudpond you two can spar and practice with one another. There's no one around here so I'm sure it'll be fine."

"Okay." Zoey said nervously.

Noah on the other hand was ready, he was happy to have a different sparring partner than Isaac. As Zoey also got herself ready she seemed determined to not let Eli down. Neither one of them seem like they were going to back down and at that moment they both clashed Noah using his wind to hover in the air and struck from above. Zoey had the same idea and grabbed water from the trees and shot up into the air with the pressure of the water. Both of them seemed relentless striking at one another seeming to be almost killing blows at this moment it was no longer a sparring practice.

Isaac and Eli saw the determined looks in their faces and moved to intervene. Eli grabbed Zoey and brought her to the ground more gently than Isaac did with Noah. Isaac had kicked Noah so hard he made a hole in the ground.

"What are you trying to do kill each other?" Eli seamed angry.

"Ow why did you have to kick me?" Noah groaned.

"Because you weren't holding back." Isaac said venomously. "Why would you go all out on a practice match you're just asking for problems?"

"Sorry Eli I just didn't want to let you down." Zoey said hurt.

"All right so now that we got that out of the way how about we have a better practice match." Eli said unimpressed.

They both nodded and took off into the air again but this time they only used half of their strengths and skills. As Zoey sent a ball of water towards Noah he sliced it into a 1000 droplets of water making it fall harmlessly towards the ground. Circling around Noah sent a volley of wind sickles towards Zoey she countered them with ease making a wall of water than pushing it at Noah. Noah saw the action and shot himself further into the air coming down on top of Zoey. Zoey having a plan of her own looked at Noah and smiled, she switched her position and ended up behind him. Noah seeing the action stopped himself and turned around quickly preparing to block an attack. Although when he looked at Zoey she was just looking at him smiling then she made a gesture with her hand it looked like she was waving at him then all of a sudden a huge amount of water came crashing down on top of him.

"That is so cold and now I'm wet." Noah complained.

"Haaa Haa sorry it was too much to resist." Zoe said laughing.

"All right you to we need to get going now or will miss the boat." Eli said grinning.

As they made their way to Cloudpond after their strenuous practice fight Zoey had plenty of time to see if she could get Isaac to lighten up. Zoey thought that if he got cooled down he might not be so hotheaded. Creating a sphere of water above Isaacs' head she grinned at the thought of him being soaked. Although before she could drop the sphere a force send her flying backwards onto the ground?

"Don't tempt me I won't hold back so don't try that again understand." Isaac said angrily.

"Yes sir." Zoey said dazed.

"You really shouldn't try to get him angry he keeps his promises." Noah said with a horrified look on his face.

"Good to know." Zoey said making sure to remember that.

When they finally made it to Cloudpond they went to get there for tickets for the ferry across to Shimmer Cliff that was South East from where they were.

"All right so we had just enough money to get the tickets so were going to need to find work when we get to the next town." Eli said disappointingly.

"Well it could be worse right at least were not stuck here." Zoey chimed in.

As they made their way onto the boat they waited patiently for it to set sail. The boat groaned and creaked as it was taking off from the port. Zoey enjoyed the water and the calm winds, although she noticed something in the distance.

"Hey Eli what's that over there?"

As Eli examined what Zoey was pointing at his face turned pale. "Isaac! We have a problem."

"What did a fish scare you?"

"That's not funny, you're never going to let me forget that are you."

"No of course not."

The both of them seemed to be sharing a private joke. "Can we get back to why I called you over." Eli said between clenched teeth. "Look over there if I'm right you can see tentacles."

"What? It couldn't be?" Isaac searched the water and found something rising out of the surface of the water. "It's a kraken."

As a squid appeared in the distance getting closer and closer to the boat Zoey could see that the kraken had at least 15 tentacles and its mouth looked strong enough to break through rocks. It was a bright blue monster and could probably go unseen in the water and strike before anyone noticed it was there. The kraken started getting closer and they could see that it was bigger than the ship, lots bigger. It could probably take down the ship without even trying Zoey thought.

"What are we going to do?" Noah came up beside them.

"I guess we have no choice if he breaks this boat were swimming the next 10 miles." Isaac laughed.

"That's not funny." Noah shivered.

"Something seems off." Zoey exclaimed and as she said that the kraken started to spitfire.

"What? Who ever heard of a fire breathing kraken." Eli screamed.

Isaac took no chances of the kraken getting any closer with his fire breath. He jumped in ready to slice it in half but Isaac didn't see the tentacle coming out of the water and it hit him hard and into the water. Isaac was dazed and sinking but then he felt as if something was pulling him up to the surface.

"Hey are you okay." Eli said lifting Isaac back onto the boat with the water.

"I never asked for your help." Isaac groaned.

"Fine, fine, I'll just let you drown next time." Eli grinned.

"Hey what's that?" Noah wondered.

"I saw something glowing in its mouth."

"All right lets change our tactics. Isaac how about you let us help you this time." Eli said sarcastically.

Isaac wasn't keen on needing help but he gave in with a bit of persistence from Eli.

"All right Zoey I want you to take care of the tentacles on the left. Noah I want you to take care of the tentacles on the right and I'll back up Isaac while he cuts it in two."

"That sounds good to me." Isaac sounded pleased to be the one having the finishing blow.

As they set out to accomplish their tasks hovering with their magic to get closer to the kraken it took everything Zoey had to keep all the tentacles in check. Noah however seemed to be managing it with ease taking down one tentacle after another. As Zoey got distracted by one tentacle to her left another one that was on here rite went straight for Eli.

"Oh no! Look out." Zoey screamed.

Eli looked over and saw the tentacle coming. Eli grabbed some water and pushed Isaac faster towards the mouth of the kraken just before Eli was grabbed and dragged under. Isaac then reached the mouth of the kraken and saw how it was breathing fire. There was a glowing red crystal in the side of its mouth and just when Isaac summoned the wind to slice it in half the kraken chose that time to breathe fire. Isaac was caught off guard and hurriedly brought up a shield of wind. Isaac started to get closer and closer to the crystal to stop the krakens' flames. Sickles of wind started to fly until the flames had stopped, Isaac went to deliver the final blow and sliced right through the kraken. As the kraken fell motionless to the water surface Zoey had dove into the water looking for Eli. Zoey looked for what seemed to be hours until she saw a figure in the distance where it was so dark you couldn't see your hand in front of your face.

"Eli." Zoey cried and lunged into him wrapping her arms around him. "Are you okay, I thought you were dead how are you able to breathe underwater?"

"I am a water follower and you haven't notice that you can to?"

Zoey at that moment noticed that she could breathe underwater. While she was in such a panic she didn't even realize that she was doing it.

"Sorry I took so long the tentacle brought me down further than I thought it would." Eli grinned.

They both started to head for the surface where Isaac and Noah were waiting for them.

"It's about time." Isaac groaned. "Our boat is almost out of site let's hurry so we can sail the rest of the way and save our magic."

"Sounds good, I just hope these two can make it." Eli looked at the two guardians that were obviously exhausted looking like they could pass out right at that moment.

They hurried to catch up with the boat and almost made it till Eli saw Zoey go down. Eli grabbed her and pulled her up out of the water.

"Zoey, Zoey!" Eli screamed in a panic.

The boat was a few feet away now and Eli could see that Zoey had only past out from the strain of using her magic for too long.

"Is she going to be all right?" Noah seemed concerned as they got back onto the boat.

"She'll be fine, we'll just let her sleep." Eli was concerned as well but tried not to let it show.

"We have a few more hours on the boat but there's no place for her to lay." Isaac exclaimed.

"Please there's a bad right over here." A voice came from a few feet away.

All three of them looked up and stared at the captain that commanded the ship.

"You're the ones who beat that kraken. I can at least offer a bad for her." The captain gestured to Zoey.

"Thank you, that would be great." Eli picked Zoey up and followed the captain to a back room near the command deck and placed Zoey on a bed.

"I'll stay with her if you don't mind." Eli gave a small smile.

"Of course." The captain nodded and turned away.

Eli sat down beside the bed as Isaac walked in. "You know you're not to blame for this." Isaac tried to sound comforting to his old friend.

"I put her in harms way how is it not my fault." Eli glared at him.

"I'm just saying. You take things too seriously she's not going to die she's just exhausted."

Eli looked away not wanting to face Isaac. "I know but I want to take care of her I don't want the past to repeat itself."

The room went quiet till Isaac spoke. "There was nothing we could do you have to accept that." Isaac turned around and walked away and Eli was left alone with his thoughts.

A while later Eli heard Zoey mumbling in her sleep saying something about a tentacle. Eli remembered how worried she looked when he finally got free of the tentacle that draged him under the water, and then found Zoey waiting for him near the surface. Suddenly her eyes opened and focused on Eli.

"Eli?... I'm sorry." Zoey started to cry.

"What? Why are you apologizing?"

"It was my fault you got grabbed by that tentacle. I didn't do my part by keeping them away, so I'm really sorry."

"No, you have nothing to apologize for. I put you in danger, I could have trained you more..." Eli trailed off and turned away not wanting Zoey to see him crying.

Zoey got up and leaned down to give Eli a consoling hug. Noah then came in and they both looked at him with embarrassed looks on their faces.

"Um...? Where almost to shore." Noah said uncomfortably and hurriedly turned around and walked away.

"Well I guess we can go and enjoy the water before we dock, are you up for it."

"Of course, you can't keep me away from water." Zoey laughed as they walked onto the deck and peered over the guardrail as they neared Shimmer Cliff.

THE DEADLY FLAME

As Natalie looked around she noticed many cages like their own many held prisoners that would most likely be sold on the black market as slaves.

"By the way my name is Natalie what's yours?" She asked the beaten boy beside her.

"It's Logan."

"It's nice to meet you; so shall we get out of here?"

"How? We don't have a key?"

"No but if you don't freak out I'll melt the bars for us okay, and everyone else to." As she looked around at all the other prisoners.

"I don't think melting the bars would be possible especially if you don't have a source of heat." Logan said skeptically.

"That's what you think, I got my ways." Natalie said with a grin.

As Natalie held onto the bars of her cage she felt the warmth of the fire in her hands slowly warping the bars. As the bars melted away Natalie smiled and moved towards Logan's cage.

"Hold on how did you do that?" Logan said surprised.

"I am able to use fire at will it's pretty neat and can get you out of tough spots although some people are scared of it so I don't use it unless I have to. That's what Sasha always tells me."

"Well then that means I will be able to help once you get me out of this cage."

Natalie looked confused as she melted the last of the bars away looking over she noticed some of the bandits looking their way with surprised looks on their faces. As they shook themselves out of the shock they started towards the two escaping prisoners.

"Well now that I'm not tied up and I'm out of that cage I guess it's my turn to shine." Logan said as the ground began to shake violently.

Natalie was impressed with the new turn of events there was only one way that this boy could be moving the earth, he was a guardian. As the bandits were occupied with trying to stay on their feet Natalie made her way towards the other prisoners' cages. They trembled in fear as she got closer holding out her hands she focused on all the cages and increased the heat. One by one the bars melted away and the frightened captives fled in terror.

"Well now that's done, I can help Logan." Natalie said as she made a tall wall of flame behind the bandits.

"Nicely done maybe we can have barbecue bandits." Logan said sarcastically.

"Thanks but I think I'll pass on the barbecue bandits."

"Ha Ha, I think you might have overdone it though."

Looking up Natalie noticed that the trees were on fire having a sinking feeling that this was going to get her into the most trouble she has ever been in before. Logan started throwing boulders towards the bandits that tried to get near them. Realizing it was a fight or flight instinct and there was no exit. Natalie calmed herself down and the wall of flames flickered and died out behind the bandits. Taking the opportunity that laid before them they ran for their lives into the woods away from the two unusual children.

"Well now that's over I should find Sasha." Natalie said frightened.

"Too late!" Sasha said angrily.

"How did you find me?"

"You're easy to find when everything is on fire I saw the smoke in the air, now let's go." Pulling out a leather strap with a collar attached to it hooking it onto Natalie's neck.

"I thought you were joking about the leash." Natalie said disappointingly.

"Ha ha Ha do you always get yourself in tough sports like this. I guess it was lucky you did this time." Logan said cheerfully.

Sasha finally noticing the boy standing there. "So I see you made a friend while I was losing my mind worrying about you." Sasha said angrily.

"Logan!" A voice came from the woods. "I felt an earthquake and I knew it was you." Leila said out of breath and panting.

"Leila is that you?" Sasha said surprised.

The two guardians looked at her and said in unison. "You know each other."

"Well isn't this a surprise it's been a long time." Leila said happily.

"Yes it has, 11 years isn't that right we have so much to catch up on." Sasha said ecstatically.

"Well then should we find a place to sleep and get something to eat?" Natalie asked groggily.

"Sounds good you two probably haven't eaten since yesterday." Sasha said while pulling on Natalie's leash and walking towards Zrin.

As they made their way into the city of Zrin Logan and Natalie started to complain of hunger.

"I know I heard you the first time." Sasha shot back. "I know you're hungry and tired but we only have enough money for food or a hotel so you need to pick one."

Natalie and Logan looked at one another and came to a decision. "We want food." They said together.

As they sat down at a Café shop in the middle of downtown they enjoyed every bit of their blissful meal.

"It's like you haven't eaten before." Leila said astonished watching both Natalie and Logan devourer their food.

As the two finished off their meal they heard a lot of noise coming from a few blocks away.

"Let's go see what that's all about." Logan said excited and energeticly.

"Shure couldn't hurt." Leila said happily.

When they got to the spot where they heard all the noise coming from they also found a lot of people gathered around.

"Who is brave enough to face the champion if you win you get to take home $25,000.00." A voice came from the center of the crowd of people.

Natalie got excited of how much they were offering and jumped at the chance. "I will!" Natalie screamed out.

All three of Natalie's companions looked at her in shock.

"What are you doing you don't know how to fight." Sasha said astonished.

"Don't worry." Natalie seemed calm as she took off the leash and pushed her way to the front of the crowd.

"And we have a challenger!" The announcer screamed out. As he looked around to find who had yelled out, he found Natalie walking up onto the stage that was in the middle of the huge crowd of people.

"What? Are you sure, you seem kind of small."

"I'm sure I can manage, and you shouldn't judge people on their height." Natalie spoke into the mic that the announcer had placed in front of her.

"I'm afraid all she heard was the amount of money and didn't think of that challenge." Sasha said horrified.

"So that thought went through your head to did it." Leila said shocked.

Sasha, Leila and Logan all pushed their way to the front of the crowd with worried expressions. Their expressions darkened when they saw who she would be facing. Natalie's opponent was big and muscular and three times taller than Natalie. Natalie was calm and smiling from ear to ear when the whole crowd of spectators were laughing. Some of the spectators couldn't stop laughing even after everyone else had settled down; to think a little girl like that volunteering to face the champion. He was called the champion for good reason he never lost and no one came close to touching him.

"Well if you're sure." The announcer seemed worried about Natalie's well-being.

"Of course." Natalie was excited she couldn't wait to spend the night at a nice hotel and they wouldn't have to worry about money again.

Natalie stepped into the ring and started to size up her opponent. "You know I'm not going to go easy on you little girl."

"I wouldn't expect you to tough guy." Natalie said sarcastically.

Her opponent didn't waste any time he charged at her and his fist crashed into the ground where Natalie once stood. "That poor little girl didn't stand a chance." He thought, suddenly he felt a sharp pain in his stomach. As he looked down he saw Natalie staring back at him.

"You know you leave yourself wide open when you go and attack someone. I'm surprised no one has beaten you yet." Natalie said wondering what kind of people he got to face.

Furious now the big man tried to kick Natalie into the air but missed and found himself on his back gasping for air. All of the spectators then started to laugh which then made him even angrier. Although the people laughing at him made him angry looking at Natalie smiling made him lose his temper. Natalie thought that she could almost see his whole body turn red. As the man tried once again to Land a blow at Natalie she evaded swiftly. It almost looks like Natalie was dancing but at the same time striking deadly blows to her target.

Logan and Leila stared at Sasha in surprise.

"Did you teach her how to do that?" Leila said in disbelief.

"No, of course not." Sasha hung her mouth open in shock watching Natalie's fight continue.

After so many hits from Natalie the big man went down. Having hit all his pressure point he could no longer moved to fight Natalie. The whole place was silent that you could hear a pin drop. Natalie had then started to walk over to the announcer that was trembling from fear or excitement she couldn't tell which.

"Um... So can I have the money now if that's okay?" Natalie said sheepishly.

The announcer handed Natalie the bag of money and the crowd broke from their silence and cheered.

"Oh my god, Natalie how did you do that." Sasha said running up to her.

"My dad taught me how to fight. Since I always get lost he thought it would be a good idea to learn how to defend myself." Natalie said with a grin. "And look now we can stay at an Inn tonight." As Natalie lifted up the bag of money.

Her three companions looked at her in disbelief.

"He was three times the size of you." Logan said still in shock.

"Yeah but my dad said the bigger you are the harder you fall. Besides he didn't seem that strong he was always wide open." Natalie giggled.

"Well since you went to all the trouble to get us that money we should use it." Sasha said happily.

"Yeah let's go to an Inn and get some rest I'm exhausted." Logan complained.

"All right there's an Inn not too far from here it's called Saffron Star Inn it has wonderful food and great beds." Leila said cheerfully.

"I thought you guys don't eat or sleep?" Natalie said confused.

"We don't or more like we don't need to we can still eat if we want to." Sasha explained.

As they made their way to the Inn people started to point and whisper looking at Natalie seeming to be so small and fragile but the little girl was actually a skilled fighter. Logan noticed all the people looking their way and thought back to the days when he lived in Sleekshield. Although the way the people here were staring seemed to be different they looked excited and curious. As they finally got to the Saffron Star Inn they rented out one room with two beds the room also had a small chair and a desk with a pad of paper and an ink pen.

"Well this room looks cozy." Natalie said yawning.

"So how long are we staying here for?" Logan asked curiously.

"Well we need to wait for the other two guardians and their followers." Leila stated.

"Okay but how long will that take?" Logan asked.

"I got a message from them a few days ago they said that they would meet us at this Inn." Sasha said reassuringly.

"Yes they should be here in the morning or afternoon so you two should get some sleep till then okay." Leila said pushing them to the bed.

THEY FINALLY MEAT

As Logan paste in the tavern of the saffron star inn he became more agitated with each step and the building started to shake.

"Logan will you sit down your causing earthquakes." Leila said annoyed.

"Sorry I just can't sit still any longer; you told me they would be here in the morning."

"I told you they would be here in the morning or afternoon."

"Then why don't we go for a walk and get some supplies for are trip." Sasha walked up with a leash in her hand.

"Okay? So what's with the leash?" Leila seemed confused

"It's for Natalie if I ever find her. I'm not sure if she's avoiding me because of the leash or if she got lost again." Sasha said in annoyance.

"That's not funny; I don't get lost that easily." Natalie came up behind Sasha.

"Great, you're here let's go shopping." As Sasha turned around and put the collar and leash on Natalie.

As they made their way through the city gathering their supplies Natalie was getting odd stairs in her direction.

"This is not fair it's humiliating and it is child abuse." Natalie sounded miserable. As she fiddled with the chain; she had got it off and wanted to show Sasha that she was capable of staying with the group without the leash. Although what she didn't notice was that they were heading to the market wear there were many people. Being tossed around and not realizing that she was being pushed further and further away from her group.

"It's your own fault; if you wouldn't get distracted all the time I wouldn't have to have bought the leash in the first place."

As Sasha looked back to stare at Natalie she was gone. "I'm going to have to weld the leash onto the collar." Sasha said with a deadpan expression.

"Freedom. See Sasha I can stick with you no problem." Nattily said happily, but as she looked around she noticed that she was lost. "You know I understand why she bought the leash." Speaking to herself.

Natalie found herself wandering around the city until she found herself in an abandoned area of the city.

"Oh, no what am I going to do now?" Natalie said in a panic.

Nattily then heard footsteps coming up behind her; so she started to run as fast as she could. Turning the corner she ran into a boy making them both crash to the ground.

"Ow, I'm sorry I'm really lost." Nattily still seemed scared.

As Natalie took in the boy she knocked over she noticed he had white hair and silver eyes.

"You better be sorry." The boy yelled.

"Hey relax; she said she was lost be a little more patient." Another boy kneeled down to see if Natalie was okay. His white eyes seemed mysterious and his silver hair looked just like that other boys' eyes.

"You know you two look like a pair." Natalie said amused.

The boy with the silver hair stepped back in shock.

"What did you say?" The boy she knocked over started to get angry again but Natalie couldn't understand why.

"Oh no." The other boy stood up and started to walk away when two other people joined them. Natalie's eyes focused on the girl with her blue eyes and Brown hair she seemed drawn to her somehow.

"Um I really am sorry." Natalie jumped up and started to back away but the boy she knocked over was too angry to let her go.

As he grabbed Natalie she got so scared his hand caught fire. He then let her go in shock and they all stared at her in astonishment.

"You're a Guardian?" The girl asked.

"What? So are you one to?" Natalie asked surprised.

"Good we found one let's get the others and go, so where is everyone?" Isaac seemed annoyed.

"Um... Yeah about that, like I said I'm lost and I'm not really sure?" Natalie looked up at Isaac he was staring her down and if looks could kill she be dead in seconds.

"I have a plan for them to find us." Natalie said pulling out her whistle.

"How is a whistle going to help?" Eli said skeptically.

"You'll see." As Natalie started to blow into the whistle.

The piercing notes blared and after blowing into the whistle three times Natalie got hit in the head.

"Ow... What was that for?" Natalie cried.

"You should know what that was for!" Sasha screamed back and clipped the leash back onto Natalie's collar.

"Well I guess it did work?" Eli said surprised.

"Yeah but what's with the leash?" Zoey wondered.

"Oh? Hey how's it going?" Sasha smiled just noticing the four other people standing there.

"Sasha wait up why did you have to run." Leila called out with Logan right behind her.

"Wow she's fast." Logan said out of breath.

"Were finally all back together again, it's like a family reunion." Leila said happily. As they came up beside them.

"Who said were family and not all of us are happy." Isaac said grumpily.

"You don't count your always grumpy." Leila dismissed the matter.

"Since were all together we should leave town quickly." Eli said concerned.

"Why?" Sasha asked wondering.

"Because we had a hard time getting here and may have a few people looking for us." Eli exclaimed.

"All right just give me a second." As Sasha melted the leash to the college.

"That's not fair." Natalie cried.

"It must be pretty bad if she had to weld it on." Zoey said laughing.

As they made their way out of town and into the woods moving west towards the mountains they noticed a man walking towards them. His close looked shredded and the man had cuts and scrapes all over his body. As they hurried to him the man fell to the ground.

"Oh no, are you okay?" Zoey started to grab water around her to heal the wounded man who was now passed out on the road.

As Zoey got to her task her companions came up behind her.

"Do you have to stop, why can't you just leave him be?" Isaac wanted nothing to do with anyone all he wanted was to get this journey over with.

"I'm not going to leave him suffering on the road when I know I could do something for him." Zoey glared at Isaac.

"Fine, whatever." Isaac walked away and sat up against a tree.

Eli kneeled down beside the men and started helping Zoey with her task.

"I'm sorry about Isaac he doesn't care for others it's probably because no one gave him a chance." Eli explained.

Zoey looked up in surprise and wondered what Eli was talking about then she thought that it was better not to pry on the matter.

As the man started to come to; Eli and Zoey stopped using their magic before he noticed that they were healing him.

"You mustn't go near the cave." The man mumbled.

"Good he's up let's go." Isaac said in annoyance.

"Don't go near the caves." The man said again.

"Why not what's so wrong about the cave?" Zoey wondered

"It's completely impassable the winds are so strong that you couldn't even get close to the cave entrance." The man said terrified.

"How about you worry about yourself and will be on our way." Isaac sneered and started for the mountain with the cave.

Since the man seemed fine now the others got up and followed Isaac to the cave. Before they got 10 feet away they could feel the wind coming out of cave entrance. It was very strong and they could see now why the man was trying to warn them. Although with Isaac in his mood he just kept on moving forward and distorting the wind to either side of him. Trying not to get left behind or blown backwards the rest of the group tried to follow as close as they could.

"Are we almost out of here?" Zoey complained.

"We just got in here." Eli laughed.

"Yeah, but I hate caves."

"Is it just me or is this wind getting stronger." Isaac wondered.

"Yeah I think it has gotten stronger." Noah tried to step forward with his own shield but got thrown backwards hitting the ground hard.

"Hey I think I saw something move." Natalie said squeamishly.

"Don't say that especially in a creepy cave." Zoey cried.

"You're a Guardian; start acting like one." Isaac yelled.

As Noah got back up they all started to move forward and came to a clearing in the tunnel. It was a big circle with piles of bones all around the clearing. With sun light streaming through an opening at the top of the cave. Even with all the sun light it was still pretty dark around the clearing only being able to see the center of the room.

"Well that's pleasant." Zoey shrank back behind Eli.

"Some things here." Leila warned.

They all looked at her with questioning expressions suddenly Zoey got her feet dragged out from under her and was starting to dangle in the air. She then saw what had grabbed her; she stared into a pare of dark red eyes and realise that it was a dragon.

THE KING

Zoey came face-to-face with an ember red Dragon with its big red eyes staring strait into her terrified shimmering blue eyes. Zoey was dangling in the air she noticed that she wasn't being held up by the dragons' claws, but his tail.

"Zoey!" Eli cried out in a panic.

As the ember red Dragon stared at Zoey and prepared to breathe his deadly flames Zoey braced herself pulling what little water she could from the air. What Zoey thought would be hot flames were actually a very intense wind that sliced through boulders. Just barely managing to keep her shield up Zoey through what little water she had left directly into the dragons eyes. The dragon screamed in pain and let go of Zoey dropping her to the hard ground but not before she saw what was on its forehead, a white crystal.

"Hey I think it's like the kraken we fought before." As Zoey touched ground and used her water to push herself as far away from the Dragon as she could.

"All right since you're all here this time why not help each other out." Isaac grind. "You four take it down, let's see what you can do."

They all looked at Isaac wondering if he was joking or not. Apparently he wasn't, Leila had made them stone seats and Isaac had a barrier protecting them in case the dragon decided to attack them.

"Talk about learning under pressure." Logan yelled.

"You had some training?" Leila smiled.

"Yeah some, it was one lesson." Logan screamed.

The Dragon didn't waste any time it started to breathe its deadly wind. Rocks started to come crashing down with the dragons rage.

"I'll stop the rocks, Noah can you make a path for the girls so they can get close to the Dragon."

"That sounds great let's throw the girls at the hungry looking Dragon." Zoey complained.

"Between me and Noah we can give you cover and make a path straight through." Logan said while holding the rocks.

Taking their chance at living through this they all moved together, Logan throwing the rocks at the Dragon keeping the dragons focus on him while Noah parted the wind. As the girls saw their opening they ran full tilt towards the Dragon.

"I'm going to lift you up okay, you attack from above." Zoey shouted at Natalie.

Nodding her head she braced herself to be thrown upward. As the water at Natalie's feet got stronger it pushed her straight into the air like an exploding geyser and above the dragons head. As the Dragon watched Natalie go up he left himself completely vulnerable to the attack that came from below. Zoey moved quickly to fill the gap striking hard at the dragons' chest. Zoey had thought that she had cut the Dragon in half with her water but with closer inspection the water didn't even make a little scratch on the dragons' chest.

"Its' scales are too hard." Zoey yelled.

In that moment Natalie had tried to aim at the dragons head using her fire like a whip. The Dragon lifted his head towards Natalie breathing the deadly wind throwing her backwards and onto the ground.

"Hey you okay Natalie?" Noah asked rushing over.

"Yeah I'm fine just a few scrapes." Natalie said gasping for air.

"I have an idea but I need your help ok we need to work together are elements can combine to make them even stronger."

Understanding what Noah was suggesting Natalie got to her feet and focused on the dragons' surroundings. Creating a circle of flames around the Dragon Noah had used his wind to create an updraft making the flames stronger fueled by Noah and Natalie. With the dragon hesitating from the flames Logan took his chance to create a spike from a boulder and tossed it striate at the dragons' forehead. The spiked rock slammed right into its head and the Dragon fell over unmoving the cave became quiet with the wind dying down.

"Did we do it?" Zoey was kneeling on the floor out of breath from all the excitement.

"I hope so." As Noah took the crystal out of the dragons' forehead.

The Crystal started to shine bright with its white light.

"What's up with this thing?" Noah wondered as the others came together.

When Isaac and Leila got closer the crystals they had on them started to glow as well. The crystals shot up in the air and started to dance around in a circle. Settling about their guardians the white being Noah's, green to Logan, blue to Zoey, and red to Natalie. The Crystal started to pulsate glowing even brighter.

"What's going on?" Sasha wondered and looked at Natalie. "Natalie? What's wrong?" Natalie had looked like she was in a trance and as she looked at the others so did they.

"I hope this isn't bad, I know where supposed to know everything but I don't even know what these crystals do or what they are for. Eli worried.

"They'll be fine." Isaac was getting comfortable sitting on the ground.

"Don't you care?" Sasha said furious.

"I just think that this might take a bit and I don't think we can move them while they're like this." Isaac explained.

Leila tried to see if Isaac was right and as she tried to get closer to Logan she got shocked pulling her hand away.

"Ow...okay, you're right we can't do anything so we might as well get comfy and wait." Leila looked upset.

"I wish we knew what was going on with them and if they're okay or if we need a doctor." Sasha said worriedly.

"What's a doctor going to do they can't even help people with simple problems; they won't know what to do about this." Isaac explained.

As they waited for the four guardians to come out of their trance for what seemed to take forever all they did was worry. As the crystals began to slow there pulsing light dimmed and the crystals embedded themselves into the four head of their guardians. Suddenly wings appeared out of their backs, pure white as they shimmered in the sun light.

"Wha..... What?" Zoey stared at Eli with a questioning look as she came out of her trance. "Why didn't you tell us what happened to the last four guardians?"

"Yeah don't you think we had a right to know that they died doing the same thing were doing now." Logan said glaring at Leila.

"Well the good thing is we can learn from the mistakes they made so we don't end up making the same mistakes that caused their deaths." Natalie said cheerfully.

"That's true but I still would have liked to know all of this beforehand. Also, now that we all have our wings we will be able to get to Gaia since it's above the city of Alumina and the only way to get there is to fly." Noah explained.

The four followers looked confused wondering what they were talking about and how they knew what happen to the previous guardians.

"It's time you tolled us the full truth." Zoey stepped forward.

"We're sorry we didn't tell you. We were hoping this time will be different the shadow master is sealed way in Gaia and he is the greatest threat we face. He was the one who started the war between the children of Gaia and the humans. We need you to finish the job; he was sealed away but that seal is now breaking. Since the seal made him weak where sure you will be able to get rid of him for good." Eli said crestfallen.

"Don't worry about it what's done is done so let's get going." Zoey started walking away with a new goal in mind.

As they headed forward they found themselves outside of the cave and could see the city of Blufron and smell the salty ocean air.

"Thank God were out of that cave." Zoey fell to the ground gratefully.

"Grow a backbone you're a Guardian. Isaac said dismissively.

"Are we near the sea?" Zoey wondered in excitement.

"Yeah we need to cross the ocean to get to our destination." Eli explained.

"Yeah but how are we supposed to get a boat. Boats don't cross the ocean from here." Isaac seemed annoyed that Eli didn't think that through.

"Relax I know the King, where good friends." Eli explained.

Everyone turned to Eli wondering how he became friends with the King of Blufron.

"How do you even know him?" Leila looked in shock.

"Well one day I was working and I found his carriage, it had been in an accident and I healed him so he was really grateful." Eli smiled.

They still couldn't believe it but if Eli had a way to get them across the ocean no one had any complaints. As they reached the entrance to the city the guards greeted them.

"Master Eli we have been waiting for you." The guard bowed his head in acknowledgment.

"Thank you, these are my companions may they come with me?" Eli asked.

"Of course, this way please." The guard led the way to the castle that was in the north end of the city which had a clear view of the port where they kept their ships.

"What's up with Master Eli?" Zoey wondered.

"Well I sent a letter to the King a few days ago when we were staying at the Double Lion Inn. I thought it would be nice if everything was ready when we got here." Eli explained.

"Well that's thinking ahead way ahead." Zoey said impressed.

When they finally got to the castle they stopped at these big grand doors that looked like they were made of gold. As the guards around the door got to work at opening them the group of guests got ushered through and the doors were closed once again.

"Those doors must weigh a lot." Sasha was impressed.

"I guess it would have to be the bigger the door the less likely it would be for someone to get through." Eli explained.

They then reached the throne room and was greeted by the king himself.

"Welcome it's been a long time since I've seen you Eli." The king seemed happy.

"Yes it has, I'm glad to see you well." Eli smiled.

"I took the initiative and had rooms prepared for you." The king seemed pleased.

"Thank you very much." Eli said gratefully.

"Of course in your letter it seemed that you could use it. Also it's getting late so you might as well take the ship in the morning."

The group bowed thankfully even Isaac swallowed his pride and bowed before the king. Then a maid lead them to their sleeping quarters. The room she had brought them to had a main Room with eight doors four on the left and four on the right. In each room there was a queen sized bed with their own bathroom.

"Now this is what I'm talking about." Natalie was excited about having her own room.

"Yeah I don't know about you guys but I'm going to bed I'm still exhausted after fighting that Dragon." Zoey complained.

"Okay, good night than." Eli said with a smile on his face.

Zoey headed to her room and fell asleep instantly as soon as her head hit the pillow.

As morning came they all prepared for their trip ahead. Natalie noticed Isaac sitting down and reading a book wondering why he wasn't getting ready.

"Where's Noah?" Natalie asked approaching Isaac.

"Sleeping" Isaac said monotone.

"Is he getting up soon?"

"No, we only hope so he's a heavy sleeper." Isaac said going back to his book.

"What if I set him on fire wood that wake him up?" Natalie asked curiously.

"I never tried that before it could work although this kid sleeps like a rock."

All right then let's try it Zoey can you heal his burns after." Natalie said menacingly.

"What you're not serious; are you?" Sasha was trying to make sure that Natalie wasn't going to do anything rash.

"I just want to get going." Natalie wined.

"Just let her do it." Isaac said smugly.

As Natalie went to Noah's room she pushed the door open and found Noah sleeping. Natalie stood at the end of his bed and concentrated on the heat in her hands and soon Noah's sheets caught fire.

"Oops my bad, I meant to get Noah. Although this will work to." Natalie was pleased with herself and walked away.

As she sat down they all waited mostly because Isaac wouldn't let anyone put it out. He was tired of waiting for Noah every morning and thought it would be nice to leave reasonably early. Soon after that thought they heard Noah scream and felt a strong gust of wind pass through the living area.

"Well looks like he's up." Isaac grinned.

"Natalie why did you set the sheets on fire!" Noah yelled.

"How rude you just assume it was me Sasha can use fire magic to you know." Natalie tried to defend herself.

"If you would wake up every morning we wouldn't have to do this." Isaac glared at Noah as he stood in his doorway.

"Fine I'm up let's go then." Noah turned around angrily.

Suddenly they heard a knock at the door.

"Come in." Eli greeted.

"Sir the boat you requested is ready for your departure." The guard saluted and waited for any further order he might receive.

"Thank you; that will be all. Don't let me keep you." Eli smiled and the soldier saluted and walked away.

As they made their way to the port of Blufron with a not so happy Noah the King was there waiting for them.

"I didn't expect that you would come down here to see us off." Eli was a bit shocked.

"Well I do owe you my life the least I could do was see you off." The King had a warm smile.

"It's been a nice visit, your kingdom is truly beautiful." Eli smiled back. "Sorry we couldn't stay longer."

"Yes it was a nice visit after all these years. Please try to keep in touch and may your journey be safe.

"Thank you; I will try my best." Eli took the King's hand and they made a silent promise.

"This will be your ship." The King turned around and extended his arm towards the ship.

The ship was big but it was only a ship that carried cargo or passengers so it wasn't as big as the other ships in the port but it would serve their purpose. The ship had to sails one in the front and one in the middle of the ship. There was also a nice sitting area and a table with eight chairs. With closer inspection the ship also had a deck below that held rooms for them.

"This is great thank you it will work perfectly." Eli was grateful.

"Of course; again good luck." The King seemed nervous he never liked boats crossing the ocean it was always dangerous.

THE RAGING SEA

"All right is everyone ready to head out?" Eli said excitedly.

"Let's just get this over with." Isaac complained.

"What's wrong don't you like water?" Natalie asked curiously.

"Not since what happened the last time." Isaac groaned.

As they set off on the ship that was so generously given to them by the King of Blfron they headed North West to Gold Breach. Then from there they would only need to head west to Gaia. They were all anxious wondering what might be on the other side of this vast ocean.

"It's just a little frustrating that were going to be stuck on this boat for three days." Logan said dryly.

"What don't you like water either? Between you and Isaac will have plenty of bad attitude going around?" Zoey said energetically.

"No, what happened to good old land." Logan said bitterly.

"Whoa you're starting to sound like Isaac." Noah was laughing at the thought.

Well we are all going to need to suck it up and pull through this." Leila said starting to get motion sick.

As the shore got further and further away Zoey started to explore their living space that would be there quarters for the next three days. Their sleeping space was small with only four beds side-by-side with just enough space in between the beds to walk through. As Zoey made her way towards the front of the boat she noticed a huge anchor with a rope tied to it. Then made her way to the back where there was a wooden bench to sit on. Staring at the water she fought the urge to jump in knowing that the powerful wind in the sales would leave her behind quite quickly. With the long boat ride that day and Zoey maxing out all the places she could explore, the day was over without her even knowing it.

"Wow I love this ship; we should do this more often." Zoey was excited as she came back to the group that were sitting at the small table that was placed in the center of the deck.

"Well you four should go get some sleep we still have a lot of traveling to do." Sasha ordered.

As the four guardians made their way to bed the four followers stood watch in case of any trouble that may occur.

The first person up that morning was Zoey and she was a bundle of energy. Of course Isaac had many thoughts of throwing her overboard. Along with her chattering mouth of how much she loves water and being on boats Isaac couldn't take anymore.

"Does she ever shut up?" Isaac was starting to get even more agitated than usual.

"Just relax." Eli didn't feel like dealing with Isaac, so he started to walk away.

Isaac had a thought that might just make Zoey quite. So Isaac grabbed Zoey by the collar of her shirt and started to drag her to the guard rail.

"Hey let me go."

"Okay." Isaac had thrown Zoey over the guardrail and watched her float away.

All Eli heard was a splash and then he turned around to find Zoey in the water and the boat leaving her far behind.

"What the hell Isaac." Eli screamed furiously.

"What? She was getting on my nerves." Isaac seemed laid back as Eli used his magic to grab Zoey and bring her back to the ship.

"You need to relax her element is water." Isaac went to go sit down at the table that was in the middle of the deck of the ship.

Eli was in Isaac's face now and Zoey could see that this was not going to be one of their normal fights. As she thought that wind and water rose and there was a heaviness in the air. They both stood there staring intensely at each other wondering who would make the first move. As this was going on the other five companions came up below deck; Sasha and Leila seemed concerned and wonder if they should jump in. After they realized the wind and water starting to tear up the ship Sasha and Leila intervened before they found themselves at the bottom of the ocean; calming Eli and Isaac down before the boat got destroyed.

"What was all that about." Sasha scolded.

Eli and Isaac were still glaring at one another and didn't seem to be in the mood to talk.

"Sorry about that it's my fault." Zoey confessed.

Everyone stared at her with a blank expression.

"Isaac had a bright idea to throw Zoey overboard." Eli sneered.

"Is that it; I'm surprised he didn't do something worse." Noah said surprised.

"I told you her element is water, why are you so bent out of shape she's fine." Isaac glared.

"It's a good thing I was paying attention than isn't it." Eli growled.

As they were all occupied with Eli's and Isaac's fight no one noticed that there was a pirate ship closing in on them. They finally realized when the pirates started to open fire on them; there were about 50 pirates on the ship. Some pirates even got close enough to board the ship pulling out there weapons and charging at Eli and Isaac. The guardians and the followers started towards the Pirates but before they could do anything Eli and Isaac put their own fight aside and took out their anger on the Pirates that ran towards them. Isaac however found another use for them using his wind magic to slice their sales into pieces and limbs along with it. Eli also taking out his rage on the Pirates pulled the water from the ocean and sliced the boat into two parts making it unsalable and sinking. As the Pirates realized what they were up against they retreated in fear some crying out in pain and others drowning. The six others watching the event unfold stood there not wanting to be the next target for their anger.

"Um Eli?" Isaac said wondering.

"What did a fish scare you?" Eli said smugly.

"I guess, what are we going to do with them?" Isaac wondered.

"What the people? Leave them."

"No, the great white sharks." Isaac said concerned wondering if the sharks will attack them next.

Looking over, Eli noticed a pack of sharks moving around the broken pirate ship. "Well it looks like its feeding time." Eli said walking away. Isaac shrugged and walked away toward the table and chairs that he was sitting at earlier.

"Well I guess we should get far away just in case they aren't full when they finish." Isaac started pushing wind into the sails.

As the day went on Eli started to feel uneasy watching the horizon.

"A storm is coming." Eli whispered to himself.

"Hey Eli you look agitated is something wrong?" Sasha said walking up beside him.

"There's a storm coming; it's a big one." Eli seemed worried.

"What are we going to do?" Sasha asked frightened.

"Nothing we can do we either hit land first or risk drowning; well you risk drowning me and Zoey will be fine." Eli said sarcastically.

The others were watching them and saw the worry on their face and went to see what was wrong.

"Were going to sink aren't we?" Isaac asked in a monotone voice.

"Most likely, unless you and Noah can put wind in the sails so we can get to land before the storm hits. Zoey and I will make it so there's less resistance from the water." Eli said confidently.

"But we still have a day and a half left before we hit land." Natalie said frightened.

"Then we better start now." Zoey said determined.

As they sped the boat up to reach land before the storm hit Zoey, Eli, Isaac, and Noah were at their limit; having been at it for two hours straight. They were completely exhausted they fell to the floor of the ship gasping for air.

"I don't think we're going to make it." Noah said looking up at the dark clouds and feeling the rocking of the boat from the strong waves.

As the storm got closer the waves got bigger and the wind blew harder. Soon the waves were so high they splashed over the railing and onto the deck of the ship.

"All right were going to have to see if we can ride this out." Eli said in a panic.

"Hold onto something." Leila screamed grabbing onto the mast of the boat which all so had a rope attached to it.

As they all tried to hold onto something trying to make sure not to get swept away by the crashing waves. A wave reached higher then the sails of the boat and came crashing down hard. The sails were in bad shape; they had lost one and the other looked like it was barely holding on.

"Here comes another one!" Zoey screamed.

The boat had taken some damage and they all knew that this one was going to be it. The way it had crashed down and broken the boat in half and they all got swept away in the current.

"Ow my head hurts." Logan groaned.

As he got up and took in his surroundings he realized he was on a beach and all alone.

"Hey! Is anyone here?" Logan screamed wondering if anyone washed up with him.

"Logan is that you!" A worried voice came from behind a pile of boulders.

As Logan started to walk towards the voice he found Leila and behind her were the rest of their friends.

"I'm so glad you're safe." Leila said through her tears.

"Why are you crying?" Logan felt a little uncomfortable.

"Because we've been looking for you for the last two hours." Leila cried. "Also my imagination got the best of me." Leila turned away and looked embarrassed. Logan wondered what she had been imagining.

"So now that were all together again let's figure out where we are." Sasha suggested.

"There seemed to be a town not too far from here. I saw lights and chimneys smoke so I'm pretty sure there's a town in that direction." Sasha pointed to the northwest.

"All right lets head there first." Leila said with a smile holding Logan close to here.

SHADOWS

"It's getting dark." Natalie stated.

"Thanks for pointing out the obvious." Isaac said irritably.

"Yes but something seems off." Eli said worriedly.

"Maybe it's because there's no people here." Logan stated.

"No that's not it; there are people here, but it looks like their hiding. There are windows boarded up and it seems like the doors are heavily locked." Eli said glaring at the houses.

As they surveyed the new town they found themselves in they noticed a heaviness in the air.

"I'm getting a strange vibe from this place." Zoey shrank back behind the group.

"Relax everything will be fine let's just find an inn." Eli suggested.

A few blocks away they saw a sign for an inn stretched out towards the street. Zoey was grateful that they didn't have to stay outside any longer.

"All right, let's get inside." Zoey said cheerfully.

They all hurried along anxious to get into a nice warm place. As Zoey past an alleyway she noticed a cat sitting on a box staring at her as she was walking by.

"Hu oooo, he's so cute." Zoey ran over to admire the little cat she always loved cats. Although when she got closer the cat stood up with its hair on end and tail in the air and heist violently. "Well that's not very nice." Zoey frowned.

"Zoey look out." Eli screamed.

As she turned around all she saw was complete darkness, and then all she felt was pane coursing through her body. Looking down the monster that looked like a shadow had stabbed her embedding it deep within her stomach. Although instead of seeing blood all she saw was darkness spreading from the shadow monsters weapon. Suddenly she fell to the ground gasping and grasping at her wound as the shadow monster vanished dying as Sasha set it on fire.

"Zoey! Zoey!" Eli screamed as she started to lose consciousness. "What are we going to do!?"

"Calm down just use you're magic to heal her; it should work." Leila suggested.

"Yaw that's right." Eli said panicked. As he started to pull water from the air and focused it into his hands focusing hard on Zoey's wound. Getting closer to Zoey, Eli saw that there was no blood but it looked like the shadow was consuming her.

"This looks bad." Eli cried.

"Don't just stand there gawking just heal her." Isaac screamed.

"All right; I'm working on it." Eli glared at Isaac and turned back to Zoey to heal her. As Eli touched her wound he felt a shock wave go up his arms and the shadow followed it crawling up his arms slowly consuming his body as well.

"Aaaaaaaa." Eli stood up and started to shake his arms round making the shadows disappear.

"What was that?" Natalie wondered stepping back and bumping into a villager. "Ow I'm sorry." Natalie stepped away as the others looked up to see an old woman standing in the middle of the street.

"The girl has been cursed." the old woman whispered. "Bring her to my place she will be safe there and I will tell you what is happening here and how to save your friend." the old woman turned around and started to walk away towards the north of town.

Everyone looked at one another wondering whether or not to follow.

"What choice do we have I can't heal her and we don't know what that black thing was." Eli paced wondering what to do.

"All right then let's trust her; maybe she even might be able to help Zoey." Noah explained.

Eli and Isaac grabbed Zoey by her arms and legs making sure not to touch the shadows that were wrapping themselves around her body.

"Are you sure this is a good idea." Logan said skeptically as they followed the old woman to her small cabin.

"Like I said we really have no choice, and Zoey's looking worse every second." Eli said; trying to hide his worry and panic from the others.

As they got to the edge of the village they noticed a small cabin nuzzled at the edge of the woods that was right outside the town.

"Won't this be fun if this is like Hensel and Gretel and were all going to be baked alive by an old woman in a small cabin in the woods." Logan said sarcastically.

"That's not funny Logan." Natalie cried, "It's scary enough out here."

The old woman had been waiting by her front door for the group that she had invited to her little cabin. As she let them in they all surveyed the room and Natalie hoping not to find a big oven for them to be cooked whole in. She was relieved to find just a small cooking fire not big enough for a person to fit in.

"Put the girl on the bed there." the old woman pointed to a small bed that sat in the corner of the room that was placed by a window. The place had only one mane room that had a kitchen living room and dining room. The fireplace was near the living room area warming the cabin. Eli and Isaac laid Zoey on the bed and went over to join everyone in the living room where the old woman had sat down on a pink armchair waiting for their attention to be on her.

"So where are we; we were aiming for Gold Breach since our ship was destroyed we ended up here but where is here exactly?" Leila said questioningly.

"You're in Ghosts Stall its three days travel to Gold Breach from here." the old woman had a quizzical look on her face wondering how they could get so far off track especially since it's to the north of them from Ghosts Stall.

"So what was that thing in the alleyway? You know don't you?" Eli wondered.

"Yes I do, and if you want the answers I suggest you sit down and listen."

Everyone sat down and made no comments and waited for the old woman to speak.

"As you might as well know the town has been cast into darkness. There are monsters roaming around and it's not just at night they come during the day as well but it's worse at night. The people are terrified and there is nothing we can do about it, although when I saw you destroy that shadow monster I knew that you would be able to do this."

"Hold on do what? We just got here and you're asking us to do this big favor for you." Sasha blurted out and stood abruptly.

"I'm getting to that, now be quite." the old woman shot back and Sasha sat back down and didn't talk for the rest of the night.

"Now as I was saying; no one can touch those monsters without dying from a disease but you can. Also the only way you can save your friend is to help us to." the old woman paused to see if her information had sunk in.

"Well I think you're wrong about that we can't touch them without dying from it as well." Logan said gesturing to Zoey.

"The cure is at the top of Tiger Mountain. Also, if you do this for our village I won't tell anyone about how you killed that monster.

"So it's blackmail." Logan said laughing.

"Great another detour." Isaac complained. "But how will this help you?"

"The medicine is at the top of Tiger Mountain and that's where the monsters lurk. The people here have tried to get the medicine but they never came back; so our people have been dying from those monsters black magic."

"Well we better get going; we should just get this over with because were already behind and the darkness is spreading. So that means there is no time to sleep." Sasha directed her last comment at Natalie, Logan, and Noah as they were drifting off in their chairs.

"Well if where going to do this I have a strategy." Logan said with a grin on his face widening as he looked at Noah and Natalie.

"Okay? Why do we need a strategy, we go up grab the herb and come back down simple." Natalie was trying to make it sound like it was no big deal so she could push it off to someone else.

"While some of us should stay here to protect Zoey just in case one of those monsters come back. So I suggest Natalie, Noah, Isaac, and Sasha go and get the herb." Logan suggested.

"Oh so you're just going to sit here and relax." Natalie sneered.

"Hey you're the one who said it would be easy to get, so good luck and don't start a forest fire with Noah." Logan laughed and got comfortable in his chair.

Natalie huffed and before anyone could speak up to talk about his plan Natalie stormed out with Sasha, Isaac, and Noah following behind her.

"Logan is so frustrating and annoying." Natalie screamed.

"Natalie wait up!" Sasha screamed. "You're going the wrong way." Natalie stopped and looked back at Sasha, Noah, and Isaac.

"Ooops sorry, okay which way are we going again." Natalie looked lost as Sasha came up in front of her and put the collar back onto her neck. "Aaaa I was wondering where that went, too bad it didn't stay lost." Natalie said disappointingly.

"All right let's get going." As Sasha pulled Natalie along towards Tiger Mountain to the west of town.

"I have a question? Why don't we fly up the mountain?" Noah grunted while hanging off the side of the mountain.

"We need to conserve our magic so we can fight those monsters then we can fly down the mountain." Sasha explained. "It will make our lives a lot easier."

"That's great and all, but what if we fall off this mountain!" Noah screamed.

"You know you three are taking the hardest route." Isaac was staring up at Noah, Natalie, and Sasha wondering when they would notice the path just below them.

"What the hell how long have you been standing there?" Noah yelled.

"Since you started climbing." Isaac stared blankly at them.

"Well, why didn't you tell us there was a path?" Noah glared back.

"I didn't feel like sharing." Isaac turned around and started to walk up the path.

As the other three jumped down on to the trail they headed after Isaac.

"Well at least we didn't have two climb all the way up to the top." Natalie was relieved to be walking up the Cliff instead of climbing it.

As they made their way up the hill towards the peak of Tiger Mountain they notice black shadows appearing further up the trail blocking their path.

"Well at least we know that we're getting closer; are you too ready?" Sasha looked at the two guardians.

"Yeah it should be easy enough they don't seem to like fire." Natalie readied herself for the fight.

"Yeah maybe we don't need to take Logan's advice we could just torch this place." Noah said with a grin.

"Geez and they call me a pie row." Natalie looked at Noah scornfully.

As they prepare to fight they moved closer together and moved faster up the steep cliff. Shadow monsters sprang out from behind boulders and below their feet. They kept moving dodging and throwing wind sickles and fireballs everywhere disintegrating their enemies instantly.

"We can't keep this up forever there is just too many of them." Sasha screamed trying to keep up with them.

"Our only hope of getting the medicine and putting an end to this is at the top of the mountain." Noah screamed back.

"Then let's blast through these things and get up there." As Natalie pushed forward and sent the biggest fireball she could conjure towards the mass of shadows. As they ran the last few meters up the hill they saw a glowing red circle it felt like it had an ominous feeling to it. The shadow creatures seemed to be protecting the glowing light and swarming in fast.

"Maybe it would be a good idea to start that forest fire now." Natalie stuttered in fear.

"What? Why, what would that accomplish?" Noah turned to find Natalie staring at him intensely. Realizing that she was very serious. "All right I trust you." Noah brought up both of his hands as did Natalie focusing their energy together as one.

"Isaac, Sasha I want you two to get up into the air." Natalie screamed out.

As they both looked at her they realized what Natalie and Noah were going to do so they took her advice and took off into the sky with their wings. When they looked down they notice the shadows advancing on them.

"Look out there getting closer." Sasha screamed and started to head towards them as the wind picked up and fueled the fire around them creating an explosion destroyed all the shadow monsters and the glowing red circle.

"Wow they used an area attack together; what teamwork." Sasha said astonished.

"What about the plant; you didn't destroy that to did you." Isaac landed right beside them staring them down.

"Relax I already grabbed it." Sasha smiled.

They all looked at her blankly. "How? When did you have time to grab one?" Noah looked confused.

Natalie laughed. "Because they're below our feet."

They all looked down and saw lush green plants at their feet and noticed that they were growing all around them.

"How are they not burnt or destroyed." Isaac wondered.

"I do control the fire, I made sure I didn't touch them. The old woman did say that these plants cure a lot of illnesses so it wouldn't have been nice if I burned them all." Natalie smiled.

"All right since we got rid of all the monsters and we got the plant let's head back so we can give Zoey the medicine." Noah started towards the cliff and brought out his wings.

"Sounds good I'm really tired." Natalie complained.

They all took off into the sky leaving Tiger Mountain far behind them.

"Now this is a better way to travel, too bad we can't keep this up for too long." Noah laughed.

"Yeah we could have just flown straight to Gaia if it didn't take up so much energy." Natalie smiled.

"Hay look I can see the cabin from here." Noah said cheerfully; flying down from the peak of the mountain.

As they landed outside the door to the cabin the door swung wide open hitting the outside wall of the cabin Logan came rushing out with boulders ready and aimed them at the unsuspecting party.

"Wow!" Noah and Natalie brought up magic shields to protect themselves against Logan's attack. "What's your problem?" Noah and Natalie screened in unison.

"What? Oh sorry." Logan brought down his boulders.

"Why were you attacking us?" Sasha wondered.

"Because they told me to keep the cabin safe. We have been getting a few shadow monsters appearing randomly and they are not helping at all with Zoey's condition." Logan slumped to the ground exhausted.

Natalie laughed. "Serves you right; since you voluntold us to get the medicine."

"Did you get the medicine?" Eli came out of the cabin looking for whoever had the herb.

"Yeah it's right here." Natalie held up the lush green herb.

"Thanks." Eli grabbed the herb and rushed back into the cabin.

They all followed, and as they entered the cabin they noticed a pot boiling on top of the fire.

"The medicine will be ready in a moment." The old woman crossed the room to Zoey. Standing over Zoey the old woman stirred the green liquid that she had grabbed from the pot on the fire and slowly put the glass to Zoey's lips.

Zoey's eyes flickered open and the old woman stopped and took the glass away. Zoey sat up and took the glass of green liquid from the old woman and drank the remaining liquid from the cup.

"Thank you, I feel much better." Zoey smiled.

"Wow! That's fast." They all said in amusement.

"Of course this herb is very strong." The old woman turned around and went to sit down on her pink armchair.

"Well now that you're better we should get going." Isaac said impatiently.

"What are you serious we just got back and I'm exhausted?" Noah cried.

"Um.... Before we do anything there's something I have to tell you." Zoey looked scared.

The room went quiet and they all waited for Zoey to speak.

KIDNAPPED

As the group took in Zoey's information they all looked frightened.

"What do you mean the end?"

"Well if we don't stop this soon every living creature in this world will die." Zoey said shakily. "In my dream there was this man dressed in black he was standing in the middle of a red magic circle.

"What? You know what a magic circle looks like?" Noah grind sarcastically.

"Give me a break it was glowing so I'm going with a magic cercal; any ways back to what I was saying before I was interrupted. He was chanting something and the darkness seemed to spread even further. Also, there were even more of those creatures as well they will definitely overwhelm us. He said his name in my dream he called himself the shadow master and all he wants for this world is darkness." Zoey looked up to see four of her companions expression changed from frightened to horrified.

"We need to get a move on then. Those monsters are relentless and they can easily overrun a city not to mention the world." Sasha looked serious.

"Well at least we were able to push them back out of this town by destroying that red magic circle." Eli said gratefully.

"Yeah now we don't have the old woman blackmailing us." Logan said cryptically.

"All right time to get going from what I have gathered there's a town north of here called Ember Pond, we should make it there in a day and a half." Leila explained.

"What are you serious!" They all screamed in in unison.

"Yes I am serious; we wasted the whole night for sleeping, and now it's time to go." Leila explained.

As she finished her sentence she noticed Natalie, Noah, and Logan passed out on the cabin floor.

"No way; you're not sleeping now get up. I will drag you there if I have to." Isaac screamed while kicking Noah. "Fine I'll grab Noah you two grab your Guardian's." Isaac gestured to Leila and Sasha wile grumbling in frustration.

"Waite when I said the name shadow master you all looked sick." Zoey jumped out of bed staring diligently with her blue eyes waiting for their answer.

"Look we don't have time to discuss this." Eli turned away and refused to look at Zoey's quivering blue eyes.

Zoey never saw that reaction from Eli before witch made her even more uneasy.

As they left the cabin they made their way north to the forest carrying their guardians while Eli and Zoey followed behind them.

Eli stopped walking and stared at the ground while the others moved further away, only Zoey was aware that Eli wasn't moving.

"What's wrong?" Zoey asked worriedly.

"I failed you as a follower I couldn't protect you when you needed me the most." Eli said glumly.

"It's okay everything turned out okay I'm all better now don't worry about it. Also, we need to watch each other's backs so we will fight together and then it won't be just one of us that gets into trouble." Zoey laughed. "Besides I know what happened to your formal Guardian was hard but I don't plan on dying." Zoey said with a small smile.

"You're right, let's get going now; I'm feeling much better thanks." Eli smiled brightly.

As they walked through the woods to the next town they were wary of their surroundings wondering where the next attack will come from. Hoping to make camp before it got too dark for them to see, they started to set up before the shadow monsters had a chance to appear. They could get a barrier ready to keep the shadow monsters at bay. Suddenly Eli saw something out of corner of his eye up in the trees. "I think were being watched." Eli said worriedly.

"You're just being paranoid." Isaac said uncaring still carrying Noah.

"Don't blame me if something jumps us." Eli walked past Isaac bumping into him making him lose his balance and bump right into Sasha. As she got pushed aside she lost her footing and fell to the ground losing Natalie as well.

"Hey watch what you're doing." Sasha glared at Isaac.

"Wasn't my fault Eli pushed me."

"Will you to stop bickering like children." Leila was standing there watching them.

"Will someone tell me why I'm on the ground?" Natalie looked dazed.

"Ow that hurt." Noah sat up rubbing his head.

They all realized that their guardians had woken up after carrying them for five hours. "Well it is about time I am done carrying you." Isaac got up and started to walk away.

"Why didn't you just leave me at the nice toasty cabin than?" Noah joked.

"If I had the option I would have." Isaac kept walking.

"Awww, now that's cold." Noah got up and walked after him.

"How did they live together for so long?" Sasha wondered.

"Well I think it was with a lot a luck and a lot of prayers." Logan laughed.

With the day dragging on they hadn't had any incident with monsters or bandits in the area although there was no life at all in the areas they had past.

"I think we walked far enough lets set up camp, Isaac and Noah can get the firewood, Eli and Zoey can get the water, Leila and Logan can get some food and me and Natalie can set up the tents." Sasha said happily.

"Why do you get the easy part of setting up camp?" Leila seemed irritated.

"Because, it's easier to keep Natalie in sight, and out of trouble." Sasha said proudly.

Leila seeded to be in deep thought "ok ya, your right. We don't want her to go missing again it's too much trouble" Leila turned and went to look for food.

"Hey I am just fine on my own." Everyone stopped and stared at Natalie blankly. "Ok maybe I have a small problem at wondering." She turned away from all the piercing stars she was getting sitting on the cold ground with her face beet red.

As they finished their tasks they all settled down in front of the warm fire. "Nice and toasty." Natalie said delighted.

"So were heading to the next town up, right?" Zoey asked confirming her thoughts of how long the trip will take.

"Right it's the town called Ember Pond I passed through their 10 years ago." Eli stated.

"It shouldn't take us long to get there if we all get up in the morning so go to sleep now Noah." Isaac said staring at him.

"Yeah, yeah okay then good night." As Noah slid into his sleeping bag.

"Am I missing something didn't they just get up a few hours ago?" as Sasha leaned up agents a dead tree.

"We need to get as much sleep as we can because with all of you we almost never get to sleep throw the night." Noah chimed in.

"Saes the one person that never gets up until 12:00." Zoey said sarcastically

The other Guardian followed Noah's lead and fell into a deep sleep in their sleeping bag. As the followers guardians drifted off to sleep they sat around the camp fire watching over them. Realizing the tension in the air Eli spoke softly "You know were going to have to do something before history repeats itself." They were all silent still thinking about Zoey's dream. "What can we do all were here for is to guide them to where they need to be." Sasha sobbed.

"Yeah, I don't want to go through that again." Isaac stared into the fire in front of him.

"Oh so someone actually has a heart." Leila mused.

Eli ignored Leila's comment towards Isaac "Never the less we still are going to protect them even if it costs me my life." Eli looked up and saw that the others agreed with his statement.

"I suppose so we lived long enough." Sasha stared at Natalie sleeping soundly in her sleeping bag.

As morning came the followers packed everything up waiting for the guardians to rise so they could continue their journey once again.

"Good morning Eli you look really agitated." Zoey said with a yawn.

"Oh no I'm fine how are you feeling this morning?" Eli asked concerned.

"I feel much better today nothing hurts." Zoey said cheerfully.

"If you get tired let me know okay." Eli stared at Zoey with a pained expression on his face.

"Okay I will." Zoey said as she took to rolling up her sleeping bag and tied it on to her pack that Eli had placed beside her.

"All right is everyone up and ready?" Sasha asked eager to get going.

"Not exactly." Natalie said kneeling beside Noah. "He's still asleep." Natalie grinned widely.

"Don't worry I will drag him along." Isaac stepped forward and grabbed the sleeping bag and began to drag Noah.

As they walked through the woods to the next town Eli had noticed little sounds and something too fast to see. "I think were being watched." Eli frowned towards the woods.

"I still think you're being paranoid." Isaac said still dragging Noah behind him.

"Yeah but you're not the brightest bulb on the tree, you still think I'm asleep I've been enjoying not having to walk." Noah mumbled.

"Are you serious!?" Isaac growled as he dropped Noah and kept on walking and didn't look back.

"Aww come on." Noah laid on the ground staring up at the sky.

"Well come on or you're going to get left behind." Logan walked by Noah.

"All right I'm coming." Noah packed up his sleeping bag and followed after the others.

"Look there's the town." Zoey said excited.

"Just don't run off we don't need any more problems like last time." Eli smiled and laughed.

"Right... I'll stay with you." As Zoey clung to Eli's arm.

As they got close to the village they saw that the trees were scorched and houses were toppled over in heaps of bricks and wood.

"It wasn't this bad when I came through here 10 years ago." Eli said shocked.

"Of course not it was 10 years ago the darkness has spread." Isaac said sarcastically.

"I can't believe the darkness got this far." Sasha said horrified.

"Let's check around and see if we can find anything or anyone." Leila waded through the rubble.

As they split up into four groups the followers going with their guardians they looked for anything they could use.

"This is hopeless; there's nothing here. All there is here is what used to be a town." Logan said while using his earth magic to lift the boulders out of the way.

"Yeah but you never know we might find someone or something very handy to take with us." Leila said while looking through what used to be a shop.

As the four groups search the town from top to bottom they came up with a pair of spark rocks that Eli found.

"We won't need those through them away." Sasha crossed her arms and stared at Eli.

"What are you intimidated by rocks." Eli grinned and shoved them into his pocket.

"No I'm just saying you have me." Sasha turned and started to leave the town but not before Eli saw her face turn red from embarrassment.

"All right let's get going we shouldn't waste any more time." Leila started to walk northwest out of the abandoned town and straight to the woods that looked like it still had some life in it.

"Strange? I wonder why this forest survived but the town didn't." Leila wondered.

"Don't think anything of it; it's pointless to wonder about trivial things." Isaac kept walking.

"It's too bad that we didn't find anything at least nothing useful." Noah said disappointingly looking back at the town.

"Yeah but at least were closer to our destination now right." Zoey said looking for the positive side.

"Well at least the next stop is Gaia; I hope you're already." Isaac went further into the woods leaving the others behind. As they ran to catch up with Isaac Zoey looked back to tell Eli to hurry up or he will be left behind. Although when she looked back he was gone.

"Um guys we got a problem." Zoey screamed at the group further in front of her. As they all looked back they realized that there was going to be one more problem to deal with before they could continue to Gaia.

"And I thought we only needed to worry about Natalie getting lost." Sasha said glumly thinking back on how many times she went looking for Natalie in the woods whenever she got lost.

As the group came back to wear Zoey was standing they started searching for Eli.

"He was dragged he didn't wonder off." Leila explained as she studied the ground.

"Then who took Eli?" Zoey cried.

INTERROGATION

Eli stood there watching the others as they walked away realizing their journey was almost to an end. He wondered what will Zoey do when it's all over will he lose her, or will he be able to stay by her side forever. Breathing a sigh of frustration he started forward, and noticing too late that an enemy was right behind him. Suddenly a cloth was shoved into his mouth and a bag was thrown over his head and tied tightly around his neck cutting off any sound he made.

Eli realized he was being carried by someone he couldn't move; his captors had tied his hands and legs together. Eli had started to panic; he couldn't move and his body was becoming sore, it felt like they had been carrying him for hours with the pain from the restraints.

"What about the others that were with him." Eli hared someone whisper.

"We had a party sent out to dispatch them." Another person whispered back.

Eli struggled in the hopes that he could get free to warn the others of the coming attack. Although all it accomplished was receiving a heavy blow to the back of his head.

"Why don't we just kill him now?" Eli heard a heavy voice say.

"Because the boss wants to know what he is and how he knew that we were there." Another deep voice answered.

A little while later Eli was thrown to the ground and the bag torn off his head he realized that they had thrown him into a cage. The cage wasn't too big that he could walk around in but big enough to stand up in. Eli spit out the gag and glared at his captives furious with the plan that they had set in motion for his companions.

"Leave him there for now till the boss comes." An older man looking to be in his 40s ordered the men around the cage.

As they locked the cage and walked away Eli got to work loosening his restraints little by little. Being cautious not to alert anyone in the camp that he was able to bend water; he used the tiniest bit to slice the leather they had tied around his hands. Coming up with a plan to take care of the bars he waited for the perfect opportunity to make his escape. With the restraints still in place but loose enough to rip off Eli surveyed the Camp and could see a woodpile to the right of him.

"That will be a good place to start." Eli thought to himself.

Eli started to look further down the camp and realized he had a ways to go. It was about 100 m to the exit and dealing with the guards would be no easy task.

As Eli was thinking through his plans an ominous man in black approached Eli's cage. "Who are you? Why are you in our territory?" The man in black glared at him.

"I'm just passing through." Eli smirked.

"Tell me how you knew we were following you since Ghosts Stall? Are you a monster a demon perhaps?" The man and black pondered his thoughts and glared at Eli.

"You were quite loud jumping through the trees." Eli remarks smugly.

The man grabbed a stick and jabbed it through the bars of Eli's cage. Eli went down on his side gasping for air with his arms still tied behind his back.

"I won't tell you anything so let me go or you'll regret it." Eli glared.

"You're not in a position to make threats." The man shot back. "Keep him locked up and guarded at all times." The man turned around and gestured to the two men behind him.

The two men nodded and saluted their superior. Eli noticed that the man in black handed something to one of the guards.

"Keys!" Eli whispered to himself and smiled. "Now if I can just break the leather restraints I can suffocate the guard with the keys, and then I could use the water around me and if I hit the other guard in the head hard enough it could knock him out." Eli started to think out his plan in more detail.

"Then all I have to do is not get caught." Eli laughed. "Easier said than done."

As Eli scanned the area he noticed two look out towers at the edge of the village near the tree line.

Eli huffed. "Of course they have look out towers; I'm going to have a hard time with this."

As darkness fell Eli had cut off his restraints that had tied his legs together. Making sure that his guards didn't notice that he had cut himself free. Slowly and quietly he moved towards his first target that heled the keys. Smothering the first guard was going well until the other became aware of what was happening to his comrade. Putting his theory to the test Eli grabbed the water around him and threw it at the other guard cutting off any sound he made knocking him unconscious. Eli moved quickly grabbing the keys and forcing them into the lock. Slowly

Eli pushed the door open carefully making sure not to let the door make any noise, and having it notify his captors. Breaking free from the cage Eli dodged into the shadows of the woodpile to the right of his cage for cover then started moving towards the exit making sure to watch for any guards along the way. Stopping behind a shack that was filled with grain Eli noticed a light across the clearing that was close to the exit he was heading for and saw a guard.

"Dam! How am I going to get past him?" Eli searched the clearing for anything that would give him cover. "I only have 50 m left to go this is ridiculous." Eli sat up against the little shack.

Eli looked at the guard again and realized that his back was turned to him. "This is my chance." Eli started to get excited as he pulled some water from the air. "Please let this work." Focusing everything onto one target trying to aim it straight at the guards head Eli let his water dart across the clearing. Seeming like minutes had passed by Eli heard a thud and knew he had hit his target. Eli realized that he was holding his breath and slowly let out a sigh of relief. "Now all I have to do is get passed those towers." Looking ahead to make sure there were no surprises and that no one had noticed the fallen guard. Taking precautions before setting out towards the exit Eli pulled out a pair of spark rocks that he obtained in the last town he came across. "And Sasha said I wouldn't need theas." Eli grinned.

Starting a little fire behind the grain shack where he was hiding behind hoping that their attention would be on the shack and not on him.

As the fire got beiger and brighter Eli herd shouting coming from behind him. As he slowly crept for more cover towards a bolder that he could not see from his cage.

Eli laughed "good thing they didn't empty my pockets." As Eli saw the guards on the two towers come over to help put out the fire Eli started forward creeping slowly through the shadows passing the two guard posts.

"Too easy." Eli was about to celebrate his escape when suddenly something fell from the trees pining him down.

In shock Eli herd someone whisper in his ear. "You know we were watching you the whole time you're a pretty crafty one especially with that water of yours." Elis expression went from shocked to anger flailing around trying to get free nocking his captive off of him. Standing up Eli surveyed the aria and realized he was badly out numbered about 50 to 1 he smiled "Like that ever stopped me before." Eli whispered under his breath.

"What was that, you are going to pay for burning down our grain shack." Before the man could reach for Eli, he felt the air starting to dry out around him like the water was being sucked out of the air itself. As he looked at their captive he had a wide grin on his face and water was circling around him the guard backed off in shock wondering where all the water was coming from he soon found himself on the ground.

Eli was starting to enjoy himself slicing through the trees knocking down the enemies that still lurked above him. Eli soon made a clearing with the trees and enemies littering the forests floor. "You should know not to mess with a stranger; you never know who that stranger might be."

Eli was ready to get back to the others but little did he know, he was still in more trouble then even Natalie could get into. Then everything went black.

THE RESCUE

"I hope Eli is all right." Zoey sniffled "I'm really worried about him."

"Will you quit your crying; Eli is a follower he can take care of himself." Isaac yelled.

"What if ghosts grabbed him?" Zoey thought.

"What? Now you just lost it." Isaac stared at Zoey with a blank expression.

"No, think about it this forest why isn't it dead like everything else Zoey shot back."

They all stared at her trying to take in what she just said.

"Well I guess it is possible considering the forest is still alive we could be going against spirits." Sasha thought through the situation.

"It's starting to get dark will need to search for Eli in the morning we won't be able to see anything right now." Leila explained

Suddenly Natalie through a fireball into the sky and lit up the surrounding area.

"What was that for; trying to scare me?" Leila looked at Natalie, although Natalie's expression was serious. "Whats wrong? Do you want to keep looking in the dark?"

"Look were surrounded." Natalie gestured to the woods.

"Aww shit; first Eli and now this." Isaac grumbled

"I hope you're all ready because here they come." Logan prepared himself.

"We don't have time for this." Zoey screamed in anger.

"Like it or not we can't go after Eli until we deal with these guys." Isaac said irritably.

"Then let's make them talk." Zoey said venomously as she charged forward conjuring duel blades of ice in her hands and struck at her opponents.

"How did she make a weapon and how did she learn to use it?" Sasha wondered.

"It was from the formal Guardian's; remember what happen in the cave with the crystals how we were in that trance for a wail. Well we learned a few things we can use their skills I can conjure the fire sword." Natali explained. "Ok then why didn't you do this before" Leila looked at her questionably. "Well we did need to practice a bit before we thought it was safe to do so also it looks like they pissed Zoey off enough that she just doesn't care." Natalie said cheerfully with a grin as she went to fight beside Zoey. "When did you ever have the time?" Leila screamed after her confused.

"Hey wait for us." Logan yelled after Natalie while creating a wooden staff and started to throw much bigger rocks and creating tremors with his weapon as he hit the weapon agents the hard earth.

As the three guardians defended themselves the followers stared in awe as they watched them take down each opponent that crossed them.

"Hey Noah, do you want to join the fun." Natalie looked over and smiled.

"No, you guys seem to be managing just fine."

"Get to work and we can get this done faster." Zoey sounded threatening.

"You sound angry." Natalie recoiled as Zoey glared at her; frightened of what Zoey would do Natalie stepped sideways on a tree root losing her balance and fell to the ground. All she saw was a man coming at her with his sword raised high; thinking that it was going to be all over in a matter of seconds. Then all of a sudden a bright white light flashed in front of her striking the man in the center of his chest throwing him to the forest floor.

"Man that was close; thanks Noah." Natalie looked over and saw what Noah had used to save her. It was a bow and it looked like he used his magic for an arrow noticing the steam coming off the string of the bow.

"You should be more careful." Noah sighed and lowered his bow.

"What is this?" Someone yelled from the attacking party.

The guardians all looked in the direction of the voices and saw a woman stepping out of the crowd. "Who are you?" The woman heist, her question was answered when the guardian's emblems started to glow.

"Oh my God." The woman whispered to herself. "I can't believe it."

They all stared at her with blank expressions.

"Okay? That's not the usual expression we get." Logan was confused looking back at Leila. Leila shrugged and started towards the unknown group.

"So what do you want from us?" Leila asked glaring at their leader.

As the woman smiled and slowly put her weapons away she gestured to the group of travelers. "Well were going to have a celebration and you are all our welcomed guests."

"You call use your welcomed guests but you ambushed us and took my friend." Zoey sneered angrily.

You could feel the tension in the air between the two groups.

"You can call that a misunderstanding we did not know that you were the four guardians. When you're emblems glowed we knew exactly who you were, please come with me and we will retrieve your friend." As the mysterious woman turned and walked away.

"Why would you attack us to begin with we didn't do anything to you; we were just passing through." Zoey glared at the back of her head. The mysterious women ignored the question and continued walking.

Eager to find Eli Zoey followed the mysterious woman with her duel blades in hand ready to strike in a moment's notice.

"So who are you and why are you here?" Natalie asked curiously.

"My name is Madison I'm the second in command of my people so there won't be any more trouble for you."

"I'm looking for my friend so if we can get a move on that would be great." Zoey glared hoping Madison would walk faster instead of talking; not taking the hint she carried on. "So your friend that you're looking for is he good with water?" They stopped at a clearing noticing full grown trees littering the forest floor.

"This is getting old just take us to your leader!" Zoey still was angry with their party and didn't want to lose any more time.

Madison looked back at her with a pained expression on her face. "We are all that's left of the children of Gaia our village is called hidden cliff it's just up ahead the elder will be happy to meet you.

"Why didn't we see hidden cliff on the map?" Natalie wondered out loud.

"Because it's hidden, and on no map." Madison stated.

Coming to a larger clearing after passing two guard posts Zoey noticed a shack meant for grain that was partly burnt and a cage a little to the right and further back from the shack. Looking closer at the cage she noticed a limp figure tied with more rope then was necessary.

Isaac noticed it as well and fell to the ground laughing and gasping for air.

"Eli!" Zoey screamed running to his side. Eli stared dully at Zoey with expressionless eyes. Zoey took in Elis condition and saw that he was beaten pretty bad with one black eye and cuts all over his body.

"Who are you?" A man in black shouted out from the crowd of people that were in the camp. Looking over Zoey saw that this man stood out from the others.

"I advise you to stay away from my prisoner." The man in black said with great authority in his voice.

"Did you do this to him!?" Zoey twitched with anger reaching her braking point. The man was taken back never being talked to in such a disrespectful manner let alone from a child.

"Then maybe I should teach you not to mess with my friends!" looking at the man in black with death in her eyes.

Raising her hands above her head concentrating on the water around her; she surrounded her opponent with the water that she had pulled from the air. Zoey's eyes sparkled a vibrant blue; the temperature slowly started to drop around them.

"Freez!" Zoey screamed out in a rage.

The water froze the man in black instantly with Zoey's emblem glowing brightly; she felt the power of the water surging through her looking at the men around the camp tempting them to try anything. The men took the hint dropped their weapons and stepped back.

"Please calm down; we will release him." Madison came running up behind Zoey to stop her from wiping out the entire camp.

Zoey stared at her impatiently as she watched her pull out the keys to the cage. Searching through all the keys she had on the small ring that she kept them on; Zoey started to tap her foot irritably. Madison looked up and saw Zoey was about ready to lose it again.

"It's right here." Madison looked fearful as she felt an icy chill coming from Zoey. Madison hastily opened the cage door in fear of being her next target and Zoey wasn't someone you wanted to mess with when she got angry.

As Zoey got to work untying the ropes and taking the cloth out of Elis mouth she focused her energy to heal all of the cuts and bruises.

"Thank you Zoey, but I think you went a little over bored." Eli grinned widely staring at the ice sculpture. "Nice ornament though" Eli laughed to himself.

"Well you look like you got what was coming to you." Isaac said smugly.

"How is that?" Eli asked confused.

"Karma, payback for all toughs tricks you pulled on me."

"Your still going on about that; it was years ago and right now." As Eli pulled the water around him and through it in Isaacs face.

"Do you want to fight frosty?!" Isaac sprung up screaming

"Or do I need to put you two six feet under again?" Lilia stared at the two of them sternly as she shook the earth beneath their feet.

"Isaac started it" Eli sneered.

"And I'm going to finish it; now stop acting like children."

Stepping back they noticed all the villagers where watching them in fear and curiosity. The tension in the air started to get a little uncomfortable for the two fallowers that had attracted the crowd. Just now noticing that Nataly was working on thawing the ice that in cased the man in black.

Nataly looked up and could see that the two fallowers had stopped bickering. "Well not like that fight wasn't important but we still need to deal with the ice sculpture I have been trying to melt it but it's too cold and thick." Nataly exclaimed looking accusingly at Zoey.

"What he had it coming." Glaring at the frozen man.

"Yeah, the rage of the water elemental great healer and comrade, but piss her off and your dealing with a tsunami." Sasha laughed while walking towards Nataly to help her out.

As the man in black got thawed out Madison took charge. "Ok so do you want to join us for a feast? We would love to celebrate the guardians return."

"Are you kidding were leaving. First you kidnap Eli then you ambush us in the forest and you almost beat Eli to death." Zoey glared daggers.

"Zoey? You know it's going to take more than that to kill me?" Eli sounded socially defeated trying to talk some sense into her before she lost it again.

As Natalie and Sasha melted the ice away the man in black gasped for air as the remaining ice around his upper body melted away.

"Good he's free, lets go." Eli turned away grabbing Zoey's hand to make sure she didn't freeze the man in black again or give Eli a reason to let her go.

"I guess your mind is made up, so at least let me show you a short cut through the woods." Madison turned and walked towards some thick brush of bushes not too far away revealing a hidden trail leading North West of the village.

Well that's handy I bet it will cut a hole day of walking" Noah grinned at the thought as the group made their way out of the village and closer to there destination.

THE TREACHEROUS JOURNEY

"Well that was a great little visit now wasn't it, but unfortunately it's time to go and get back on track." Natalie said cheerfully hope she would relieve the tension in the air. Even though it was so much fun watching Zoey go nuts.

"Yes back on the road to Gaia but along the way all four of you are going to need to learn how to control your emotions and weapons." Leila glared at the four guardians. "Expeshily you, Zoey." Leila turned and started to walk away.

"I thought Zoey would be exempted from that because she can already make one hell of a cold snap." Natalie giggled.

"You're never going to let me forget that are you?" Zoey glared expressionless towards Natalie.

As they left hidden cliff Zoey looked back one last time to make sure that the man in black wasn't going to fallow them. Although if he did; she would put him in his place quickly.

"Now then since Zoey has already demonstrated her skill with her magic and weapons we will start with one of you three." Isaac scanned the other three guardians.

"What! But you already know what I can do; you trained me for ten years." Noah looked frightened remembering the endless training with Isaac in the mountains."

"Yes. But you can hardly fly let alone use your magic properly." Isaac stared at Noah waiting for him to reject the fact.

"I'm getting better." Noah looked away embarrassed.

"Alright lets pair you up, Zoey your with Natalie and Noah your with Logan; try to use only your weapons this will also help you control your emotions wile welding your weapons." Eli explained. "Logan, Noah your first."

"Sounds good; I have been wanting to fight with Noah to see how strong he really is." Logan grinned sounding very confident.

"Really... there's no rush." Noah shied away from Logan's' arrogance wishing it wasn't Logan he got to spar with.

"Alright, whenever you're ready." Eli grind expecting to see an all-out sparing match between the two boys.

As they got ready Logan bent to the ground placing his hand on the soft dirt and pulled out his staff making it appear like it was coming out of the earth itself. On the other hand Noah had made his bow appear out of thin air. As they emerged out of the woods they reached a barren waist land and the boys started their practice match. All around was darkness and holes with dark energy; it looked more like really thick tar as black as a nights sky. As they boys kept exchanging blows the girls wondered off to investigate the black holes that were all over the ground as far as they could see.

"Girls carful, you're going to fall in." Eli warned.

"I think you still worry too much; we'll be fine." Zoey smiled and made sure to watch Natalie very carefully.

As the match was still going on behind them they herd the boys clashing and screaming at one another something about a fowl. Before Zoey when to look back she felt a hard shove and found herself and the three other guardians plummeting towards the black pool that she was just observing.

As Zoey opened her eyes she saw a familiar scene of the river by her old home; her favourite place to sit and watch the river rush by.

"What? How did I get here, Eli? Is anyone there? Hello." Looking around Zoey noticed two people standing at the top of the hill smiling. They both looked very happy to see her but very worn down with gray hair. They looked familiar to Zoey and then she realized why. "Wait! Is that.... Mom, dad you're alive!" she screamed in excitement and ran to them, all of a suddenly the scene went up in smoke; in the blink of an eye her family was gone, the two people that she had called mom and dad were gone. Looking through the ruble of her home she notices her mother sitting it her rocking chair staring at her mumbling.

"What? What's wrong, mom come on let's get out of here weirs dad?" Zoey was panicked.

"You did this to us, You Did This To Us, YOU DID THIS TO US." The old women repeated getting louder and louder as blood started to spill from her eyes and nose.

Zoey started to back away in terror moving towards a corner of the room sliding her back agents the wall; she sat down and started to cry as the room got darker all around her.

"Zoey?" She heard a familiar voice call out. "Who's there?"

"Don't tell me you forgot me already." Eli suddenly appeared in front of Zoey.

"Eli!" Zoey cried.

"Zoey remember when we first met and you followed me. I want you to follow me one more time." As Eli held out his hand to Zoey.

Zoey nodded and smiled as she took Elis hand and escaped the darkness in her heart.

As Noah opened his eyes he felt dazed staring up at the blue sky he realised he was no the ground. Righting himself he then saw a cabin that he knew all too well it was the one he grew up in as he started towards the cabin he herd crying in the distance farther into the woods. As he went to investigate he found a women with silver hair and she held a basket. Taking a closer look Noah realised that there was a baby in the basket.

"Wretched child." As she placed the basket on the forests flour and started to walk way.

"What? No wait don't leave me as Noah tried to catch up the vision faded to black and he found himself alone in the dark.

"Accursed child, you were never meant to be borne." Noah was trying to drown out the words.

"Noah?" a voice whispered softly. "Come on I didn't spend ten years raising you for you to regret the past; let's go follow me.

"Natalie." A voice called out softly.

Natalie spun around to see were the voice was coming from with the sun shining upon the little cabin in the woods were she would play all day, and at the door of the cabin were her parents.

"Mom, dad you're here." Natalie ran towards them with tears in her eyes. As she reached the steps to the cabin her parents disappeared. "Why didn't you listen, it's your entire fault." Her mother screamed.

As the vision became darker and she could no longer hear her mother's voice; Natalie was left alone with her thoughts and tears.

"I'm sorry; I'm so sorry." Natalie sobbed.

"Natalie? Do you really think they would say that to you to the little girl that they loved so much." The voice spoke delicately. "Don't you remember what your father told you?"

Natalie looked up and saw a bright light ware she found Sasha waiting for her. "Alright then let's go and make them proud of you okay." Sasha turned away with a smile and lead Natalie out of the darkness.

As Logan opened his eyes he found himself in the village he hated so much but still had a lot of memories involving the homes he used to live in. He reminisced about all the people that took him in nice caring people but in the end his nice dream of a loving family came crashing down all around him. He found himself staring at all the people that took him in including the children that were also living in the home.

"Sabotage, murderer!" The voices screamed out.

Logan couldn't take it anymore so he curled up onto the floor and put his hands over his ears.

"It's alright now Logan you have me." A gentle voice broke through the darkness. Looking up he found Leila standing in front of him with her hand reaching out to him. "Let's find a new home together." Leila smiled brightly as Logan reached up and grabbed her hand.

"Ow what happened?" Zoey realised that Eli was dragging her out of the pit of darkness.

"Are you really sure I don't worry enough." Eli stared at Zoey out of breath from diving after her into the pit of darkness.

"I'm sorry I didn't think that would happen." Zoey smiled sheepishly.

"That's alright at least it got us to our destination faster." Isaac looked around at their surroundings and found that they had been teleported from one pit of darkness to another. "Looks like someone wants us hear faster as he peered towards the city of Alumina.

Zoey looked around and saw that the other guardians were still past out on the hard cold earth. As she inspected the city from where she stood it was directly ahead, it looked dark and run down from what she could see. As the others got up and joined her they realised they had more work to do then they planned.

"How did we get all the way hear?" Natalie wondered.

"It was a teleportation spell." Eli announced. "What I don't get is a spell like that takes a lot of energy. I think he's mocking us he doesn't think we can beat him."

"You mean the shadow master? How do you know it's him?" Noah wondered."

"Because he's the only one I know that can use a spell that strong." Eli stammered.

THE LAST STAND

As they approached the city of Alumina they noticed cocoons littering the streets and sticking to buildings.

"What happened here?" Zoey started walking towards a cocoon that was leaning agents what looked like to be a clothing stall; although it was over grown with weeds and rubble lying about. As she looked closer at the cocoon Zoey shrieked and jumped back.

"Will you be quiet!" Isaac hissed.

"Sorry, sorry...It's just that theirs a person inside the cocoon."

"What?" Isaac walked up closer to the cocoon. "So that's what happened to all the people." Isaac grimiest.

"The only way that we are going to be able to fix this and make it rite is to finish what we started, let's get up to Gaia and beat the shadow master at his own game." Eli looked determined.

The four guardians gazed up towards Gaia with fire in their eyes Nataly more literally then the others.

"This is our last stand; this is where we end it." Zoey said passionately while bringing out her beautiful white wings and sored upwards towards Gaia.

As they all flew up towards the floating city of Gaia their emblems started to glow along with the crystals embedded in their forehead. Reaching Gaia's Cliffside Noah started to hear a low hum of energy; being the first one peering over the cliffs edge Noah saw a magic mesial coming strata at him. Moving quickly he reversed his flight and dropped down slightly missing the magic mesial; falling fast he tried to gain back his balance but before he could right himself he crashed strait into Zoey sending them spiraling out of control.

"AAAA!" Zoey screamed in panic righting herself and landing on the nearest platform.

"Are you two okay?" Eli asked nervously, as he came down to land beside Zoey.

As the others realised that it wouldn't be safe going up they all joined Zoey, Eli, and Noah on the platform.

"Do you think we can tunnel up?" Natalie mused.

"We could give it a try; couldn't hurt right." Logan smiled confidently. As Logan slowly drilled through the hard earth he created a passage way for them to navigate through. As they pushed forward Zoey fell behind thinking to herself.

"It's almost time, isn't it?" Zoey thought as she touched the blue crystal on her forehead.

As they made their way through the cavern Logan slowly started to ascend getting closer and closer to the center of Gaia.

"So how do you know where we are?" Natali wondered.

"I can feel the vibrations on the island, and that tells me were we are. We'll pop up just behind the runs of this old temple.

"Okay so the direct approach didn't work." Natalie smiled.

"You can say that agene; Noah almost lost his head and slammed into me really hard." Zoey glared dully.

"We can't just sit here and do nothing." Eli screamed in frustration.

"Were not we are making a tunnel underneath the city. That isn't nothing, it's a lot of hard work moving all of these rocks and tunnelling without making a sound." Leila glared angrily at Eli.

"Well we are moving too slow." Eli muttered. "Alright; we still don't know what we are going to do."

"That's easy; all we have to do is get to the center of Gaia and we will be right in the middle of the battle field." Logan glanced back and grind.

"That's great; so your volunteering to get your head cut off first then." Zoey said sarcastically.

"Well if we're going to end up dying who wants pocky?" Natalie smiled widely pulling out a box of pocky.

They all stared at her blankly. "Were did you get that?" Sasha was confused.

"I got it when we were at Hidden cliff; you weren't paying any attention so I wondered off and someone was selling them. I thought it could be my last meal or treat." Natalie giggled.

"Wow way to be a downer." Logan said grimly "Don't worry so much I'll hide us behind a rock wall; we won't die." As they kept on moving.

Zoey watched as the group moved ahead and thought to herself about the grim conversation. "I hope your right." Zoey looked crestfallen.

As they reached the surface of the floating island of Gaia they hid behind a rock wall that Logan had strategically brought them up behind. As they all looked around they noticed it was a barren waist land worst that the city of Alumina. There was nothing but rock and a dense dark Ora. Peering around the rock wall they saw a man in black standing in the middle of a black magic cercal chanting.

"His back is turned to us and he's distracted; let's get him now before he knows were here." Logan whispered as he bolted out from behind the rock wall towards the man in black.

Before anyone could stop him they found themselves following behind wishing that Logan would be more sensible.

"Foolish boy, did you not think that I couldn't feel you digging through the ground." The voice sent shivers through all of them stopping them in their tracks. The voice was venomous and cold knowing that he meant biasness. As the dark figure turned around he sent a dark beam of light spiraling towards Logan. Moving swiftly Leila tackled Logan to the right of the beam just barely missing Leila's shoulder.

"Aaa so the followers are also here, good I can pay you back instead of the ones who sealed me away and to do that I can slowly take away your guardians and then it will be your tern next." The shadow master grind widely and sadistically as he was imagining his plans and the pane that he would inflict.

As Noah notices an opening he sprang to the air trying to get as much force as he could into his attack heading strata down to attack him from the air. The shadow master seen him coming and forced Noah's wind back at him sending Noah behind him opposite from the others.

"One more." As the shadow master grabbed Zoey and Eli with a dark magical rope and tossed them to his right. With all of them tossed in opposite directions of each other he started to cast a spell with a dark magic cercal surrounding him; as he finished his chant they were all frozen in fear and before they knew it they were tossed backwards far away from each other.

"Good now I can pick them off one at a time; this will be too easy." He started to laugh menacingly.

As Zoey slowly opened her eyes she realised It was quiet and dark and all Zoey could feel was despair and pain. Suddenly a light started too bloom in the distance. "Who's there?" the light felt worm and inviting. Zoey could start to make out a shape of a woman with a blue crystal on her forehead with light blue hair and sparkling white eyes. She reminded Zoey of the river she used to visit back in her home town and how the river made her feel calm and secure.

"Everything will be alright; trust in yourself and you will succeed." The women smiled gently.

"How were all separated there's no way we can beat him he's to strong we need to make a plan but I don't know where to start looking for the others." Zoey trailed off.

"Don't despair; don't you know his weakness?"

Zoey looked confused so the women continued. "He's alone and you have friends to help you."

"But were so far apart how will we ever be able to fight together."

"Don't you remember my advice." The women smiled. "Water is ever flowing."

Zoey looked shocked. "That was you back when I had my first vision."

"Yes I have always been with you same goes for the others you will never be alone. Now one more thing before you go would you mind giving Eli a message for me. "

Zoey listened intently then the space flooded with light and the women disappeared. As she opened her eyes she noticed Eli staring down at her with tears in his eyes. "Zoey! Thank god you're ok!" Eli screamed and hugged Zoey.

"Flora." Zoey whispered.

Eli sprang up in shock. "What did you say?"

"Flora she was your former guardian she wanted me to give you a message."

Eli looked tense wondering if Flora was mad at him for all these years.

"She said living in the past won't take you anywhere but living in the present will take you everywhere. She also told me how to use telepathy so we can talk to the others." Zoey looked pleased and felt like a weight had been lifted.

Eli took in what Zoey had said and smiled. "Then I guess we have some work to do."

As Zoey started to concentrate she connected to the others. "Hollow can you all here me?" Zoey felt there consciousness waver as they jumped from the sudden sound of her voice.

"Wow neat trick when did you learn that?" Logan wondered.

"Never mind that now, Logan I need you to shake the ground and keep it shaking so the shadow master can't find us. Noah I need you to through some whorl winds around through him off his game. Then we'll all move in on him and attack all at once we need to be in sync with each other."

"How did you not come up with this plan before we got our asses handed to us?" Logan said disdainfully.

"Well I would have if some moron wouldn't have jumped in so quickly." Zoey shot back.

"Oh right." Logan got very quiet.

They all got to their tasks pulling out their weapons and getting closer to their target. Moving swiftly they cot the shadow master off guard not expecting them to be so close, as he did send them in opposite directions.

The shadow master grind. "Foolish children do you think you can beat me." He notice Natalie and Zoey and wondered weir the other two were. As he tried to move to attack them he notices that he couldn't move his feet. "What is this!" he peered down and realised that his feet were frozen to the ground. He then realised too late were the other two were he was surrounded from above and below and with the girls at either side. As they swung at him he grabbed their weapons and the flowing energy in their weapons got thrown back at them sending them sprawling to the ground but he was too slow to doge the boys coming at him from below and above. Noah sent an arrow strait in to the shadow masters shoulder wail Logan jammed his staff into his stomach. Gasping in pain and nursing his shoulder he fell to his knees.

"All right you guys got him." Zoey smiled and they then notice that the girls didn't get away unscathed. Zoey had a wound to her side and Natali was bleeding from her head.

"Are you two ok, can you keep going?" Logan rushed over in concern.

"Yeah, not a problem." They both smiled and raised themselves to their feet.

"Good then we can continue and end this." Eli walked up behind them with the other three followers.

"Are you ready, let's do this." Isaac grind and closed his eyes and started to concentrate. The others followed soot. "Restraint!" they all shouted in unison and chains appeared from the magic cercal underneath their feet binding the shadow master in place making him unable to move.

"Go do it now; destroy him before he gets free!" Eli screamed.

The four guardians focused their remaining energy to the crystal on their forehead sending the energy in the form of a person realising that the people were the former guardians. The shadow master was bathed in light and disappeared from existence. With all the energy flowing from them Gaia had been restored with grass and flowers growing every ware and Alumina brought back to its former glory with life spreading every ware.

Drifting through the wind the followers heard the faint voices of their former guardians. "Thank you for everything." As a worm feeling came over them. Everything was bright for a short wail and as the light faded they saw their guardians passed out on the ground and not being able to feel any life energy coming from them.

Isaac sat in the corner in the room in a wooden chair reading one of his books. Waiting patiently in a room at the Pacific Flower Inn that was located in the city of Alumina.

"Hay, how are they doing?" Eli walked in with a grim expression taking in the room with the four beds that held the four guardians.

"They're the same as they were three days ago." Isaac didn't miss a beat. Eli had come in every day for hours waiting for them to wake. As they sat there talking they suddenly heard a low grown coming from one of the four beds. Their heads shot up with surprise because not once in three days have any of them starred in their sleep. They then notice Noah sit up rubbing his eyes and looked around the room. Noah notice Eli and Isaac siting in the corner of the room. "Hey guys how's it going where are we?"

Isaac dropped his book on the ground and stood up abruptly and walked over to Noah sitting down on his bed and raped his arms around him.

"Wow what's wrong with you." Noah was thrown off from the hug and notice that Isaac was also crying. "Hey you're freaking me out." Noah blushed.

"What do you know you do care? Under that facade there is a big softy." Eli grind. He then notices the other three guardians coming too in excitement he rushed over to Zoey puling here close. "I thot you would never wake."

Zoey smiled. "You should have more faith." As she got up out of bed. "Come on I want to see the city."

"What you know where we are?" Logan looked confused as everyone headed outside.

They all looked around with the sun pouring through the clouds and people bustling about. The city was beautiful and safe once agene the way it should be.

Printed in the United States
By Bookmasters